I0680309

AMERICA:
LOVE IT OR GET THE HELL OUT

FROM THE GREATEST GENERATION
TO THE GUTTER GENERATION
AND HOW TO DESTROY A POLICE DEPARTMENT

ROBERT E. LEE ELLIOTT

KANGAROO PUBLISHING

Table of Contents

This book is divided into three sections...

Section One: the background of the author, the myth of Due Process and how unscrupulous lawyers can destroy a person's life

Section Two: How some lawyers are nothing but well dressed thieves with a license to steal and the destruction of a police department

Section Three: Ride with the officer on his tour of duty and understand the struggle between life and death and how easily you can be robbed by the system that's suppose to protect you

Dedication

This book is dedicated to all those qualified people who would have made a worthwhile contribution to society and the police department but through no fault of their own lacked the gift of being at the right place at the right time and knowing the right people.

Foreword

This book is intended for mature adults and if you get easily offended then put the book back on the shelf for someone else to read. No fancy words are being used to impress anyone and it's written to be easily understood by the common layman. It's not necessary to have a dictionary by your side to define words that I use. I write for the down trodden, the forgotten and those that have lost their zest for life. Those that have nothing but the shirt on their backs. I'm the author that doesn't give a rat's ass about the elite and their fancy high living way of life. Most rich or well to do people can't relate to the poor and average person and has the habit of looking down their nose at them in the false belief that they're better then them.

My writings are based on my own personal experiences in life and I don't search the internet trying to find information that I don't know anything about or if it's true or not. You don't have to be a rocket scientist or a Harvard graduate to understand where I'm coming from. You can rest assured that I didn't just ride into town on the back of a cabbage truck so relax. Actually the truth of the matter is I did ride into town on the back of a coal miner's truck when I was seven years old. To really understand the author and the events that cast his character in stone, you must read his other book "Kangaroo Justice and Well Dressed Thieves With a License to Steal." From my childhood to manhood it has been one mountain after another to climb and a life of hard times.

One thing you must always remember if you don't remember anything else. Don't ever pass judgment on another person until you have walked in his shoes. In the case of myself I was born dirt poor and will probably die dirt poor due to the so-called Rule of Law and Due Process which can and does completely destroy a person's life when administered by crooked ass lying lawyers and indifferent judges. It can strip a man of his wealth, his reputation and everything he holds sacred. If you're able to walk and enjoy all the wonders of life and nature be thankful for it because a lot of people can't and do everything just to survive. I firmly believe that everyone was put on earth for a particular reason and it wasn't meant for us to understand or question. Never take life for granted because it can be taken away in an instant and for no apparent reason. One thing for sure all of us came into this world with nothing and that's exactly the way we'll leave it.

Introduction

To start with I've never been placed in awe at someone's position in life. Every big cat so to speak puts his pants on one leg at the time just like I do and I'm not impressed. Some of the biggest nit wits that I've ever seen walk around with their nose in the air thinking that they're someone special. I always picture that person sitting on the toilet taking a dump and for some reason he doesn't look very distinguished. Always look at a person for what they are and certainly not for what they think they are. Being a chief executive officer (CEO) is usually the biggest fraud possible in large companies. Talk about being overpaid, they rip off companies for millions of dollars by simply blowing smoke up the asses of the company boards. In any operation the higher up a person goes the less actual work he or she does. They rake in all the money while the poor workers on the bottom do all the work. Well, you probably get the idea of what I think of all the deadwood on top of any operation.

In my twenty five years with law enforcement I have discovered that most promotions within the department are nothing but popularity contest and is one of the primary reasons for the demise of a police department, but we'll have plenty of time later to fully explain how that comes about.

Before we get down to the mud slinging I think it's appropriate that everyone knows where the author is coming from and what his future may hold for him. The author is just an 84 year old cripple with plenty of health issues that will no doubt be his end in a few more years or sooner. I suppose you could say that I fall into the middle class now, but that was decided by mother luck.

As you will find out my family was dirt poor, hard-working and had nothing but that's a story that will come to light later on as it's addressed. I retired from the Dade County Police Department located in Miami, Florida on December 27 1985 after twenty-five years of honorable service. The last twelve years was served as a uniform police lieutenant in the uniform section. I hold an Associate of Arts Degree from Miami-Dade Community College, a Bachelor of Science Degree in Criminal Justice from Florida International University and a Master of Science Degree in Management from Biscayne College also located in Miami, Florida. I served eight years in the United States Naval Reserve and hold an Honorable Discharge which I'm proud of to this day even though I wasn't treated fairly by the Veteran's Administration when I needed help. I went to the Veteran's Hospital in Asheville, N. Carolina to get some medicine and was almost thrown out the door and informed that I wasn't entitled to anything. In retrospect, I should have enlisted in the Army for six months and dished beans so I could qualify for all the benefits offered by the Veteran's Administration. I enlisted in the Naval Reserve for eight years attending drills, going to boot camp in Rhode Island and serving time on two Destroyer Escorts, the US Tills and McCleland; chipping paint, painting dept. charge racks and K-guns while participating in war exercises at sea didn't mean didly squat to the Veteran's Administration. When I transferred over to the Construction Battalion, better known as the Sea Bees, and pouring concrete in the islands for the construction of officer's quarters didn't mean anything to the Veteran's Administration. Attending drills and going on military cruises wasn't given any consideration either. I look at all my diplomas hanging on my office wall, including my Honorable Discharge from the United States Navy, and wonder if it was all worth it because my government doesn't seem to think so.

As a young boy in high school I had a paper route with the Miami Daily News and a route with the Miami Herald until I graduated from Miami Edison High School in 1953. Then I worked for the Merita Bakery as a mechanic's helper, the Art Craft Cabinet Company and six years with Southern Bell Telephone Company as an underground cable helper and installer. After six years with Southern Bell I was accepted for employment with the Dade County Sheriff's Office in Miami and there was were the reality of life hit me in the face.

I don't believe in fairy tales or make believe fictional stories. I only write from my own true experiences and nothing else. I don't google everything under the sun or search the internet for something to write about that I don't have personal knowledge of. If I see something on the internet that is proven true and people should know about I'll mention it. Anything that is reported by the news media requires verification because they have fallen into the liberal trap of fake news. In other words with me you get what you see.

The more you read the more you'll understand why I strongly believe that some people should not be entitled to a trial and how a proud police department can be destroyed by so-called progressive thinkers and political correctness. I have discovered that it doesn't do one bit of good to try and change a person's mind when it comes to politics. Just bear in mind and save yourself a lot of aggravation, it's almost impossible to fix stupid.

The Story

You will notice that I'm not the accepted type of person that usually writes books because I tend to be very direct in my feelings and if I think someone's a nit wit I'll tell them so without any hesitation. I don't make any effort to impress anyone and write in simple language so it can easily be understood by everyone. You don't need a dictionary to look up words because if it's over two syllables it's probably a curse word and I wouldn't use it in the first place. Later on I'll get into the question of crimes and punishments and why I don't believe that everyone is entitled to a trial. I'll give examples why I believe it and it will give you something to think about. First, let's start from the beginning. I was born in a small rural town in the hills of Northern Alabama. Talk about being dirt poor my family lived it and if it wasn't for polk salad, rabbits and squirrels we would have most likely starved to death. The only way my father could make a living was by making whiskey and being a bootlegger because the only people surviving in town were bootleggers and preachers.

The school house consisted of one big room divided into six sections for the first grade through the sixth grade. There was only one teacher and she taught all the grades at the same time. There was no such thing as a cafeteria and if the student didn't bring his lunch to school he didn't eat. There was no such thing as welfare, food stamps or a school bus. We had to walk to school because someone owning a car was a rarity. During harvest time school would be dismissed at noon each day so the students could go and work in the fields with their parents. My mother, my two older sisters and brothers would work in the cotton fields until dark. Since I was the youngest and no one was left at home to watch over me, my mother made me a cotton sack to wear and had me follow behind her as she picked cotton. She would purposely miss some cotton pods for me to pick. On many days I would see my mother's fingers bleed from the sharp cotton pods but she never complained. My two oldest brothers joined the Navy when the Japanese attacked Pearl Harbor and my dad went to Florida looking for work. I love it when I hear some kid these days complain about not having a car to drive, a cellphone or more designer clothes to wear to school. They have no understanding of material things because they've never had to do without. When I was a young kid back in Alabama my mother made my clothes out of empty flour sacks and I was happy to get them. I never got anything new and store bought to wear and felt lucky to get my older brother's hand me downs to wear. The young people of today have no idea what it is to do without and live through hard times. Our old farm house had no electricity or plumbing and the only heat in the house was the fireplace and at night the only light we had was kerosene lamps.

On Sunday night we all would walk a mile down the highway to attend church. The only light in the church was by kerosene lamps sitting on shelves along the wall. It was apparent to my parents that as long as we lived in that little town of Beaverton none of us would ever amount to anything and it was decided to sell out and move. The entire place with eighty acres sold for one thousand dollars. My mother hired a coal truck driver by the name of Mr. Muntz to move us to Miami. He charged mother eighty dollars to move us and piled everything we owned in the back bed of his truck. My mother was the only one able to sit in the cab of the truck with the driver. The rest of us rode in the back all huddled together under the tarp. Our journey certainly looked just like the television show The Beverly Hillbillys and it was a long and tiring trip for all of us. I'm sure we must have amused a lot of people seeing us and looking like refugees from a concentration camp. My mother had to be the bravest mother in the world and the rest of us had to be the dirtiest kids in the world from riding in the bed of a coal truck covered with a large tarp. My mother got to ride in the cab of the truck but the rest of us had to ride in the back underneath the tarp. The morning that we arrived we stopped at Bakers Haulover next to the ocean and none of us could believe what we were looking at. The beautiful palm trees, the ocean that none of us had ever seen before and the huge sandy beach. Everything was so beautiful and strange to me. I knew at that very moment that I was going to love the state of Florida. I had never seen a lighthouse and such tall concrete buildings on Collins Avenue. We finally got settled into a small wooden car garage with dirt floors until mother found us a nearby house that we could live in. I went to the nearby Little River Elementary School that I could walk to without crossing a busy street. One day as I walked to school I passed a building that was called a funeral home which was strange and unknown to me because back home in Alabama there was no such thing as a funeral home. When my grandmother passed away her body was laid out in the living room of her house while the rest of the family ate in the dining room and celebrated her life. After the eating and socializing they'd put Granny into a wooden casket and take her to the church house next to the cemetery. After the singing and preaching they'd take Granny outside and lower her into her final resting place.

After moving to Miami my dad got a job at the Tropical Awning and Shutter Company as a carpenter. After working there for a couple years he finally got a job with the Florida East Coast Railroad Company and my mother got a job at The Miami Delux Laundry for twelve dollars a week. I never knew that we were considered poor until I overheard my first grade teacher say it to her son who was in my class. It was a cold day and she told her son to take off his sweater and give it to me. He couldn't understand why he had to give his sweater to me and that's when she told him that it was because I was poor. When I got home my mother asked me where did I get such a beautiful sweater and I told her that my teacher gave to me because I'm poor. I will never forget the hurt look on my mother's face when she knelt down in front of me as tears tolled down her face, hugged me and told me that we weren't poor because we had each other and that was all that mattered.

I was so skinny and looked so bad that they gave me a job in the school cafeteria for lunch and twenty five cents pay every Friday. That twenty five cents looked like big money to me because back home in Alabama I never saw any money much less money of my own. With the money that my mother got from selling our place in Alabama my mother put some money down on a brand new place located on North West forty six street. What a mansion, it had an indoor toilet, running water, electric lights and beautiful wooden floors. To me it was a mansion fit for a king and I thought for sure that we must be rich and certainly not poor to live in such a beautiful house. I'll never forget my mother paid four thousand two hundred dollars for the place and the monthly payments were twenty five dollars.

My two oldest brothers were in the Navy and I would watch mom get on her knees every night beside the bed and ask the Lord to please watch over her boys and bring them safely back to home. She would always ask Jesus to have his Guardian Angels watch over and protect them from harm. If my mother isn't an angel in heaven then there is no heaven. I only ask my Lord and Savior Jesus Christ to save my soul and permit me once again to see my dear mother in heaven.

The war finally ended and my brothers came home and I continued my journey to manhood. During my journey I never swerved off the path that my mother so carefully placed me on. She always told me to treat other people the way I wanted to be treated and that good and right would always prevail. My life has taught me that what seems to be a tragedy today may well turn out to be a blessing tomorrow.

Always live your life according to the Ten Commandments and your life will be built on a strong moral foundation and hard times will only build good character.

Out of high school I became influenced by an older brother who was a Deputy Sheriff with the Dade County Sheriff's Office. I soon realized that my interest and heart was directed to law enforcement. After working my way through numerous unrewarding jobs, Merita Bakery, Southern Bell Telephone and construction companies I finally got hired by the Sheriff's Office on October 10, 1960 and that's when the interesting part of my life begins. I went through class eighteen of the police academy and hit the streets with my shiny new badge and a rule book on how to enforce the law. It didn't take long for me to realize that the teachings of the police academy and the real world was two different things. In the large majority of time a police officer's contact with the public is potentially confrontational and required a great deal of self control on the officer's part. In the early days of my employment with the department there seem to be a lot of respect for a police officer but over time it was turning to a strong feeling of disrespect. During that time I went back and researched my job application and job description to see if getting my ass kicked was part of the job description. I've always believed that a person has to have a degree of fear toward authority in order for any person to exhibit any degree of respect for it. By this I certainly don't mean that a citizen should have fear of physical abuse from an officer, warranted or otherwise but from the court system.

Over the years I could see and witness the slow breakdown of law and order. It seem like it was becoming routine for officers to be assaulted and even shot. For any police department to be effective our criminal justice system has to operate under two primary concepts, the punishment has to be swift and sure and the punishment has to fit the crime. Being able to communicate with people is really job effective and I learned early in my career to talk to people on their level in

5

order to be understood. I always showed respect to people that were respectful to me but on the other hand if some punk talked trash to me I'd unload on him and bury him with trash talk so we could understand each other.

I personally have very strong objections to our justice system and how well it serves criminals. You always hear people say that we are a nation of laws and everyone must abide by the law. That happens to be a lot of bullshit because I see lawyers and politicians getting away with violating the law constantly and nothing is done about it. Hell, even the big shots with the Federal Bureau of Investigation appear to be crooked and corrupt as hell and everyone just stands around scratching their ass wondering what happened. The Democratic leadership is so busy trying to stop President Trump they are falling over each other. It's apparent that they endorse socialism and couldn't care less about the welfare of American citizens. Like the book title says "America love it or get the hell out" and if the Democrats care more about illegal immigrants then the American citizens then it's high time for them to get the hell out of America. All of the legitimate politicians need to get off their ass and do something about the runaway corruption in government and stop the liberal assholes from trying to destroy our president.

First, I'd like to make it perfectly clear that I'm a strong supporter of the National Rifle Association (NRA) and the second amendment of the Constitution but I'm not so open minded that my brains have fallen out onto the floor. I firmly believe that no one should be able to purchase a firearm at a gun show, on line or at a dealership unless they're at least twenty one years of age. Regarding automatic weapons such as the AR-15 they should be outlaws for the general public because their only intended use is for killing people. I refuse to accept any explanation from so-called hunters that they need such a weapon to go duck hunting. For myself I don't believe in killing any animal and calling it a sport. Anyone that has the mindset for killing any animal is apparently mentally disturbed to some degree and simply shows that he or she does not value life. The medical field has shown that any young person that enjoys the killing of animals has a serious pending mental problem which will show itself in later years. It has been shown that it is a childhood trait of a serial killer which is recognized by the medical field. To me they're nothing but gun nuts and deserve to be hunted down in the woods by other so-called hunters so they might be able to understand how an animal feels. I personally spend a great deal of money on apples and corn to feed the deer that comes in my yard.

At present that politicians just stand around scratching their ass trying to figure out how to stop the school shootings and keeping guns out of the hands of the mentally ill. All mass shootings are not done solely by the mentally ill but out of pure hatred of another person's culture or occupation such as a police officer. At present we have the tail wagging the dog regarding the question of keeping guns out of the hands of the mentally ill. One wild radical solution to the problem would be to have a law that required everything that tries to buy a firearm produce evidence that they have no criminal past or present mental issues. Talk about upsetting the ACLU, the NRA, politicians, gun nuts and so-called hunters, all of them would be running around with their hair on fire screaming that the sky was falling. If there was such a radical law in existence all those murdered students at Stoneman Douglass High School in Parkland, Florida would still be alive today.

Next is just one glaring example of why I don't believe that everyone should be entitled to a trial. The Parole Board in California just issued a parole to a black prisoner that murdered three police officers while one officer was lying on the ground begging for his life. That officer was shot twenty five times and the paroled prisoner was the one that administered the shots to the officer's head. This scumbag prisoner served forty one years in prison and got married while in jail and knocked his wife up three times while still in jail. The United States

Supreme Court had ruled that depriving a prisoner of some female ass was cruel and unusual punishment so all the male prisoners were permitted to have the ladies come into the prison and service them. That way the male prisoners could have the pain and suffering of having no ass resolved. With the Supreme Court ruling prisons became nothing but over flowing whore houses. It certainly would appear that the prisoners had the life of Reilly considering all of the extra activities that they were able to enjoy in jail. When a person is incarcerated for an extended period of time he becomes institutionalized and you can't drag him out of jail and the good life.

I personally feel that for justice to be done that sack of feces should have been hung in the public square and left there to rot while the buzzards picked his worthless bones clean. That low life sorry bastard did not deserve a trial and have taxpayers support him for forty one years. No doubt he became institutionalized and preferred prison life and especially getting all the ass he could handle. Who the hell would want to be on the outside scratching for a living when you can enjoy life on the inside just sitting on your ass? Enjoying three meals a day with lots of desserts, a law library, movies, pussy, basketball court, weight room, television, game room and most likely all the smuggled in pot that you can smoke. No more having to get up and go to some stinking job.

Sometimes I think of throwing a brick through the window of the local police station so I can get my ass into the jail and good life. At least I know I'll be able to get laid by some horny lady whenever I please and that's a lot better than having to chase them down on the outside.

When the second amendment was drawn up by the framers of the Constitution it was put there to provide a militia for the new government of America. It certainly wasn't drawn up for the benefit of hunters and gun nuts. Doesn't the term "minutemen" ring a bell and tell you something? During those early years of our country there was no militia to speak of to provide protection of our declared independence from foreign and domestic powers. The second amendment provided America with a civilian army in time of need. Scholars have argued and rightfully so that the sole purpose of the second amendment was to guarantee that the civilian militia could keep and bear arms for the protection of our country. Our forefathers were more concerned about providing for our defense then worrying about duck hunters and hunters in general.

Sometimes liberal minded people make knee jerk statements regarding the National Rifle Association and/or the second amendment and have no idea what the hell they're talking about. For instance there are thousands of misguided high school students marching around screaming about the so-called sins of the National Rifle Association showing their ignorance. They actually blame the Association for causing school shootings which is nothing but a lot of senseless immature bullshit. Walking around bitching about something will always attract a room full of lawyers. If any kind of emergency occurs where someone is hurt and injured within a few minutes lawyers will trample each other in order to get to the injured person first. That way the lawyer will be able to sue anyone and everyone that may have contributed to the injury. Lawyers consider an injured person as money in the bank and they know how to squeeze money out of a turnip.

Before I forget I have some advice for every property owner that's happy where he or she is living. If you're happy where you're at then stay there and don't even think about moving and getting into a more expensive neighborhood. I moved from where I was quite happy to a restricted neighborhood and after spending a small fortune on a new house I soon discovered that I was surrounded by pricks that wouldn't mind their own business and made my life miserable. I have one neighbor that is totally paranoid to the point that he has installed cameras to watch everyone and installed two large gates in front of his house. It's obvious by his actions and taking pictures of everyone driving up the road that he doesn't have both oars in the water. On top of that he has an alarm system in his house that's always going off. It's apparent that he needs some kind of medication or therapy to get his head out of his ass.

I was assigned to work in a mental ward when I was in law enforcement and I know a loony tune when I see one and this particular neighbor needs some kind of psychotic drug to help him because I don't think mental therapy alone would do the trick.

I have another neighbor that doesn't have any balls so to speak and his wife runs the show and tells him what to do without any hesitation. She has a habit of sticking her nose in other people's business, including mine. Then I have another neighbor that thinks she's a real bad ass and she's nothing but a real fat ass. She turned out to be one lying bitch and has convinced herself that she's another Ma Barker and the meanest bitch in the valley. Actually she's the ugliest bitch in the valley and should look in the mirror and behold the truth. She's one of those people that think they're smart as hell and don't know their ass from a hole in the ground. In my humble opinion the hole in the ground has more sex appeal then her fat ass. It's like actor John Wayne once said, "Life is tough but a lot tougher when you're stupid."

The more you read the more you'll be convinced that we're living in the gutter generation because stupidity is rampant throughout our country. The America of today is certainly not the American I grew up in. Can you believe it? I saw some dip stick woman on television saying that any word containing "man" should be changed because it degrades women. Just looking at her and listening to her babble I realized then that she needed something more than changing a name. For example she said that the word "mankind should be changed to peoplekind." The more she talked the more it because obvious that she had her head stuck in her ass. What happens to some people's reasoning ability is beyond me. Chuck Schumer and Nancy Pelosi fit the model of Ma and Pa Kettle perfectly by their reasoning power. The more I listen to nit wits the more I give up on the human race.

I'm certainly not a big fan of Russia's President Vlatimir Putin but Like I've said before he made a statement that I fully agree with even though it goes against our present day justice system. He stated that "not everyone should be entitled to a trial." I also believe that under certain circumstances dealing with some felonies and capital murder a person should be denied a trial. Recently two police officers were having lunch when a subject walked up and shot both of them to death. If that low life scumbag had lived why would it be justified for him to have a trial and have a half dozen lawyers trying to get him off the charge at taxpayers expense? In my opinion and to serve justice he should have been drawn and quartered by four horses until he was in four pieces. It would have made a good half time show in a football stadium at half time for everyone to watch. Even now under current law if a murderer is found guilty and sentenced to death the immediate family of the victim should be given the opportunity to administer the death penalty.

When our forefathers drew up the Constitution dueling was not a violation of the law but with passing of time it had to be outlawed for good reason. It's the same with trials, circumstances change and rules need to be changed in order to maintain justice as we know it. In colonial days the attitude and actions of people were quite different then they are now. The numerous ways and means or murdering people today wasn't even dreamed of back then. In my opinion if a person is caught in the commission of a murder or apprehended and the evidence of guilt is overwhelming and beyond the shadow of any doubt, that accused should not be entitled to a trial. A panel should determine the person's sentence and not waste taxpayer's money on a senseless trial. In a lot of trials they're nothing but a waste of taxpayer's money and only serves as a way for lawyers to get money and do everything they can possibly do to set the defendant free and escape justice. If O.J.Simpson was caught with Nicole's severed head in his suitcase should he be entitled to a trial? He was guilty as hell and the team of lawyers did everything they could possibly do to have him found not guilty. Please bear in mind that being found not guilty doesn't mean that a person didn't commit the crime. His lawyers didn't give a rat's ass if he killed ten people. They knew that they could milk him dry of all his money and that was the only thing that mattered to them. Each lawyer had a particular assignment in the trial. One lawyer was to discredit any witness including the police as was done to Detective Furman on the witness stand. Another lawyer was to muddle the blood evidence and any other evidence found on the scene. Each lawyer had their assignment to set Simpson free regardless of how they had to do it. Marci Clark of the prosecution made a justice killing blunder when she didn't object to Simpson trying on the glove found on the scene. It was obvious that the glove wouldn't be easy to get on because it had been soaked in blood and had shrunk. As one lawyer stated, "we didn't win the case, the prosecution lost it."

In our system of so-called justice you can only get that amount of justice that you can afford.

In 2006 on a television interview Simpson readily admitted that he was at the crime scene and witnessed a man by the name of Charlie killing both Nicole and Goldman. He said that he tried to grab the knife from Charlie and that's how his finger got cut. If anyone can believe his tale of bullshit then they need to have their head examined. The sorry son of a bitch murdered two people and got away with it due to a racist jury that wouldn't convict their hero if he had murdered ten people on the fifty yard line during half time at the Super Bowl. The concept of our legal system seems logical but in reality it simply doesn't work like it should due to most of the lawyers having no morals when it comes to right and wrong. Our country is run by unscrupulous lawyers who would rather steal from people then work. Out system of justice is flawed and needs to be changed as in my particular case where I was unjustly robbed of everything by a lying bitch lawyer and two brain dead judges.

I have mentioned it before but if it's mentioned fifty times it still wouldn't be too much because people must start to understand prison life. If a murdering bastard is convicted of multiple killings he'll most likely be sentenced to life in prison without the possibility of parole. After a few years in prison the asshole will become institutionalized and would rather be in prison then back on the streets scratching for a living. After the Supreme Court ruled that it was cruel and unusual punishment to deprive a man of female sex prisoners can get more ass in prison then they ever could on the streets and it's free. After a few years you couldn't drag a prisoner out of jail and deprive him of the good life. The last thing he wants to hear is for the Warden to tell him that he's a free man and to leave the prison. Hell, sometimes I think I'd be better off in prison because I'm sick and tired of being kicked around and blamed for everything. As a child I was born into a dirt poor family and after all these years lying ass lawyers have put me back into poverty.

Fear and respect go together like a horse and carriage. Without one you won't have the other. That's why criminals don't have any fear of the justice system. A shithead punk will spray paint someones car and a church house because they know that if they get caught and arrested by some miracle the courts won't do anything worthwhile about it. No worry, vandalize to your hearts content because the courts really don't give a rat's ass what you do. A judge represents the final nail into the coffin of justice and most should never have been appointed to a judgeship in the first place. How can you expect a judge to be unbiased when he was practicing law twenty years before becoming a judge? I've come to the point where I wouldn't trust a lawyer or judge any further then I can throw their ass.

During my robbery case I found that the two judges I appeared before didn't care what I had to say and most of the time didn't even recognize my presence in the court room. I had the feeling before the first word was spoken that I was on a sinking ship without a fighting chance of saving myself from being mugged and robbed by the court. As President Trump said, the system is rigged and I got a front row seat at my own robbery. I found myself in my situation because of a lying female lawyer in Fort Lauderdale, Florida who was constantly leading a circuit court judge around by his nose and getting everything she ask for without any effort. I would receive a subpoena to appear in court ten days after the hearing was held. It wouldn't surprise me if she wasn't bending over and letting the judge show her where the wild goose goes. Something had to be going on for her to be treated so good without limits. She is known as Douche Bag Mary and looks like a douche bag.

That lying bitch continually sued me for twenty years for everything she could think of starting in 1998 to 2016. She specializes in representing trailer trash and probably uses the top of her desk for something other than writing on if you get my drift. The judge that she was filing affidavits with was advised numerous times that they were being filed under perjury but that didn't seem to matter. The judge was told that she admitted to me on numerous occasions that they were lies but that was my problem not hers. For some strange and unexplained reason the judge even refused to question the truthfulness of the affidavits being filed by Douche Bag Mary. Good old Douche Bag. She ain't very pretty or smart but she does know how to work a judge. To receive such special treatment from the judge it would really surprise me if she wasn't bending over and catching that wild goose.

I've often said that humans breed like flies and it's estimated by 2050 there will be nine billion people on earth. It looks like the average person is going to screw theirselves out of a place at the dinner table.

The only hope of controlling the population growth is for people to start using their head more if you get my drift.

Most lawyers suck big time as far as I'm concerned and like I said I wouldn't trust one as far as I can throw his or her scroungey ass. Lawyers will do anything to get a client off and now they encourage jury nullification. Regardless of the convicting evidence jurors are told to always vote not guilty. Just for example look how it freed O.J. Simpson for slaughtering two people. Jury selection is very important to the defense lawyers and they make every effort to select the ones that aren't too bright. It really worked good for the defense during the Simpson trial because the jury was obviously racist and wouldn't even consider any of the state's evidence. When the verdict was announced the black communities cheered and celebrated showing their racism and hatred for the so-called white establishment. The lives of the two innocent victims weren't even considered. The intelligence level or I.Q. of the jurors had to be so low that it wasn't even on the chart. As I said before each defense lawyer was assigned a duty and the one assigned for picking the jury apparently knew how to recognize ignorance and was a sure way of being picked for the jury. The main object for the lawyers was to cast doubt on any and all testimony given by the prosecution. It became obvious that the seated jurors were a bunch of morons. Then of all things the presiding judge and his lack of ability to control the court room was another mistake. To me he reminded me of what a Japanese fighter pilot would look like bombing Pearl Harbor.

Considering the judge, the jury and the defense lawyers the prosecution didn't have a snowballs chance in hell of finding Simpson guilty. The state could have produced Nicole's severed head in Simpson's suitcase and the jury would have still voted him not guilty. Again I must remind you that just because the defendant is adjudicated not guilty doesn't necessarily mean that the defendant didn't commit the crime.

I have always contended that every new born baby should have their DNA taken at birth as well as taking the DNA of everyone living in the country.

No one should be excluded including green card holders that come into the country to work. Everyones DNA should be recorded in a national data bank for DNA. Not only would it discourage criminal behavior but it would go a long way in resolving and solving criminal cases that are open and pending. They just recently identified a serial killer and rapist that had raped forty five women and murdered twelve women. I believe he was known as the green river killer in California and was seventy years old when identified by DNA and charged with rapes and murders that occurred forty years ago. Between DNA and fingerprints committing the perfect crime involving rape and murder would be hard to come by.

As a detective in a large and proud police department I learned early that when investigating a crime the first place you look is within the family circle. Then you expand the investigation to all of the immediate and surrounding neighbors. After that you determine who are the friends of everyone within the family circle and run background checks on everyone that surfaces. Most crimes of burglary, robbery, assault and theft are usually solved by someone handing up the subject to save their own ass on something else that involves them.

I caught a rapist in Miami, Florida simply by writing a speeding ticket to a motorist. In lieu of the summons he handed up the subject that raped a woman in the neighboring county of Broward. He stated that he would have the subject in his car Saturday night and would run the traffic light at North West 27th avenue and 54th street at exactly eight o'clock on their way to Key West. I was sitting on my police motorcycle at the intersection at 8 o'clock and sure enough he approached the intersection at a high rate of speed and ran the traffic light and the race was on. He was driving at such a high rate of speed it was all I could do to catch him. The rest is history, he handed his friend up for a twenty dollar ticket. Scratch one rapist.

Since my own robbery case and seeing how lawyers and judges operate I've become to love animals far more then most humans. The entire system of criminal justice should be reviewed and changes made to meet the needs of society. There should be limits on how long a congressman can sit on his ass collecting $174,000.00 a year for doing nothing. At present a congressman can stay in office until he's ninety years old and drooling all over himself. If we don't get term limits then the country will continue down the road to hell and I'll keep saying it until hell freezes over. Parole Boards underminds justice in the strongest terms. Parole Boards only invites bribery to everyone on the Board. Being a board member invites corruption and the elimination of justice. Money can and does sway a member to vote for paroling some particular prisoner. If some people think that it doesn't happen then they're naïve as hell and probably still believes in Santa Claus. In my humble opinion I strongly believe that when a defendant is sentenced to a term in jail he should have to serve every-day of it. If he is disruptive in jail and a trouble maker just add more time to his sentence. If a prisoner conducts himself like an animal then treat him like an animal. The system is so caught up in rehabilitation that it has lost sight of punishment. They always say let the punishment fit the crime and punishment should be swift and sure. Both concepts sound good but if you really believe and think that it represents our justice system then you don't know what the hell is going on. Parole Boards are for the benefit of criminals and serves no useful purpose for society and should be abolished before more cop killers and murderers are released back on the streets. If some sorry ass bastard kills a police officer then by law the killer should receive the death penalty.

As a police officer I experienced what it means to literally fight for your life. One early morning I went to the aid of another officer who wouldn't respond to his radio. When I arrived at his location I observed him fighting with a black male and I joined in as quickly as possible to help restrain the subject. In the struggle all three of us fell to the ground as the other officer yelled "Elliot, he has my gun." I saw the gun in the subject's hand and was holding his arm as he was screaming "I'm going to kill your white ass." When we fell to the ground I broke my ankle and as soon as we got the subject under control I had to go to Parkway Hospital. He was arrested for the initial charge of prowling but another charge of resisting arrest with violence was also added. The sorry bastard tried his best to kill both of us but we were saved that night by the fickle finger of faith. Later I learned that he worked as a security guard at the 167th street shopping center and was shot to death by someone that he was trying to arrest for shoplifting. Quite frankly I was somewhat delighted to hear the news. Sometimes when people make their bed they have to sleep in it.

I have found that there's a time to love and a time to hate. A time to laugh and a time to cry. A time to be happy and a time to be sad but most of all a time to live and a time to die. Have you ever known someone that couldn't get over something? I have a neighbor next to me that's one of those people. The way he conducts himself, talks and acts there's no doubt that he's mentally unstable and potentially dangerous. I worked in a mental ward for awhile during my employment with the police department and I can recognize a loony tune in a heart beat. Most of the immediate neighbors have finally realized that he needs help because he's totally paranoid on top of everything else he does.

I have learned one thing for sure. Anyone going to church on Sunday morning singing praises to the Lord and goes home Sunday night and plots how to harm someone is not a Christian in my book. I have a neighbor that claims to be a Christian and can't spell the word.

Here recently the former vice president Joe Biden, attended some kind of rally at the University of Miami and stuck his foot into his mouth again. He started bad mouthing President Trump again and said that if he heard Trump belittle some woman, he'd take Trump outside behind the gym and beat hell out of him. Well a news flash, the only thing that Biden can beat is his meat and he's probably still carrying on a love affair with Mrs. Palm and her five daughters. This is the same Joe Biden that stood on a national stage when he was running for president against Obama and told the entire nation that Obama wasn't qualified to be president. Later on national television he stood by his statement and repeated that Obama wasn't qualified to be president. After that remark Obama selected him to be his vice president which shows how much intelligence Obama had. Good old Joe he spent the next eight years sticking his foot into his mouth and his nose in Obama's ass.

Joe Biden seems to be real effectionate toward women by the way he touches them on stage while someone is making a speech. During the time he debated Sarah Palin during the run for the oval office he certainly didn't hide the fact that he thought she was real nice. Sometimes it appears that some in the Republican Party don't support President Trump the way they should as shown by the Bill that President Trump had to sign in order to get funding for the military that Obama let go to hell. The Bill consisted of two thousand pages in length and no one was given enough time to read it. I understand that it funded Planned Parenthood by giving it five hundred thousand dollars. President Trump was against funding Planned Parenthood because it aborts ten thousand black babies each year. Murdering that many unborn babies doesn't seem to bother Chuck Schumer, Nancy Pelosi or the Democratic Party because they do everything possible to continue funding the organization. I personally can't understand why the black people aren't raising holy hell about thousands of babies being murdered. For myself I hope that anyone that murders an unborn child goes straight to hell where they belong. Too many women use abortion as a form of birth control and I hope they burn in hell for it. Too bad if it hurts someones conscience but abortion is just another word for murder.

Some of the young people that are participating in the marches for whatever cause don't even understand what they're marching for. They can march until hell freezes over and it won't accomplish a damn thing worthwhile but if it makes you feel better then keep on marching. Listening to some of the students making speeches it's obvious that they don't know their ass from a hole in the ground. Looking at some of the signs they were carrying it made me determined more than ever that the only way anyone will get my gun is to pry it out of my cold dead hands.

The rotten Bill that President Trump had to sign in order to fund the military didn't include didly squat for the border wall. One time the Democrats considered giving 1.6 billion for the wall but now in order to destroy Trump even that offer doesn't exist. President Trump has the option of declaring a national emergency and getting the money to build the wall. He should stop wasting his time with Crying Chuck Schumer and Grease Rack Pelosi and declare a national emergency. The figure of 1.6 billion dollars for the wall is nothing but a drop in the bucket. The Democrats will do everything they can possibly do to destroy President Trump and win the 20/20 election. It's not about the wall they have turned it into a political football in an attempt to deny President Trump the election in 20/20.

I have suggested that President Trump should start a national campaign for donations for the wall and tell Nancy and Chuck to kiss his ass. I'm glad to see that Trump has shut down part of the government and hope that he doesn't cave in when the Democrats start their bitching. Now it should be obvious to the close minded Democrats that our country desperately needs the border wall right now to keep thousands of undesirable people from storming into our country unchecked. At present we have thousands of people from shithole countries in Central America invading our borders and have no respect for our laws. They invade our country and assault our Border Patrol Officers with bricks and rocks. They call it a caravan and ride on top of the train boxcars through Mexico to get to our country. Their intention is to overwhelm our immigration authorities and enter our country whether we like it or not. Of course immigration lawyers are running over each other to tell all of them how to lie in order to seek asylum. The more I see of lawyers the more I agree with what Shakespeare said a long time ago. "The first thing we need to do is round up all the lawyers and get rid of them." Shakespeare knew what the hell he was talking about and it would do the country a great service now if we took his advice.

Again if a national campaign was started for the wall donations and everyone that voted for Trump sent in one hundred dollars he'd have enough money to build three walls forty feet high and have enough money left over to hire hundreds of Border Patrol Agents. In doing so he could place the wall question on the back of the Democratic Party where it rightfully belongs.

I'm always reminded of our flawed judicial system with a revolving door that only encourages lawlessness. During my career with law enforcement I would occasionally work vice and arrest the same prostitute two or three times during my eight hour shift. Sometimes they would get out of jail and beat me back to the area I was working. It reminds me of a funny incident that occurred one evening during my shift. A prostitute walked up to a tourist standing on the sidewalk and asked him if he'd like a blowjob? The tourist responded "No, I still have three weeks of unemployment benefits coming to me."

One evening two subjects committed an armed robbery, one subject was arrested and the other one fled into a nearby wooded area. While we were searching the wooded area for the other subject the first one had bonded out of jail and returned to the area to watch us searching for his friend. Over the years I could see a lose-lose attitude developing in myself and other officers. The seeds of this attitude were planted in the police officers by things such as affirmative action, political correctness, incompetent supervisors and formation of different organization within the department that served only to divide and disrupt the operations of the department. Any organization that has the word progressive in it's title usually reflects a racist leadership and civil rights lawyers at every turn so be aware. Between those self serving organizations and outside interference from the county manager's office the police department will slowly be destroyed. Dade County Florida had a county manager that thought he knew more about how to operate a police department than the highly respected E. Wilson Purdy. Director Purdy was known throughout the country for his expertise and ability. Totally incompetent people were being promoted to supervisory positions to satisfy "affirmative action" and the situation only continued to grow worse. Those supervisors had no understanding of police operations and had no management skills so the department operations continued to go to hell. They didn't have the ability to know the difference between being a realist or a idealist. During this transition from a kick ass department to a kiss ass department it became nothing more than a public relations minded department. All this came about because the empty suit county manager fired one of the most capable police administrators in the country that ever passed through Dade County Florida, E. Wilson Purdy. The county manager apparently suffered from narcissism and lived under the impression that he knew more about everything then anyone else. If anyone ever needed a good ass kicking it was the empty suit and empty headed county manager. He was so well known for being a jerk he would sneak out the back door and down the stairwell to avoid anyone seeing him.

It wasn't long before a supervisor with the Sheriff's Office that the county manager was held bent on destroying started dating the manager's secretary. Apparently the secretary had a lot of influence with the county manager because he appointed the police supervisor to be the Director of the Dade County Sheriff's Office. The new director and county manager were made for each other because they were like two peas in a pod. The new director was nothing more than an errand boy for the manager and played the role of a parrot. Whatever changes in the department that the manager wanted his boy gave it to him. The county manager was running the department and the director was nothing but a figure head and the only thing missing was his "balls."

The following pages is the retirement memorandum that I submitted to Director Bobby Jones on December 15, 1985. It is the exact wording and nothing has been added or deleted so you can fully understand my frustration seeing the department finally being destroyed. Even though this memorandum was written thirty three years ago my opinion has not changed one iota.

MEMORANDUM

B. L. Jones, Director   December 15, 1985
Metro Dade Police Dept.

Robert L. Elliott, Lieutenant   Notification of Retirement
North East District

With mixed emotions I tender this as notification of my pending retirement which will be effective December 27, 1985.

I'm leaving the department with the knowledge of knowing that I gave my best to the department and the citizens of Dade County. For the past few years I have lived and worked under the full realization that due to my ethnic background, my promotional opportunities have been greatly diminished.

Hopefully in the future, the young dedicated officers on the department will not be burdened by the policies implemented by you and Mr. Stierheim. Your extreme affirmative action program has elevated some totally incompetent personnel to needless upper management positions in the department.

Too often there seems to be no correlation between promotional opportunities and ability. You have accumulated a track record of promoting personnel based solely on race, sex and ethnic background in "Carte Blanche" fashion totally disregarding merit and ability. You have circumvented the civil service rules in the specific case of Major Lonnie Lawrence and with the apparent blessings of the county manager.

Hopefully one day the county commission will come to realize that Mr. Stierheim was not the appointed Messiah that came to lead people from his imaginary bondage. History will reflect the devastating results of his Moses syndrome.

The policies that you and Mr. Stierheim implemented under the guise of affirmative action have all but destroyed the excellence and motivation that was once the wellspring of the department. The administration of the department remains deaf and indifferent to the voice of justice and the county manager's attitude parallels that of King George III.

Your extreme affirmative action policies have resulted in gross and blatant actions of reverse discrimination and the quality of management and leadership has suffered drastically in the process. The department's professionalism, individual integrity, personal motivation and etc. has steadily declined since the county manager decided to implement his own personal philosophy regarding affirmative action through you. His philosophy combined with your lack of individual innovation and compassion has bankrupt the department in the areas of morale and excellence. The department is saddled with some upper management personnel that are direly lacking in formal education, an understanding in human behavior and are typical examples of the "Peter Principle."

History will reflect that the department and sadly enough, the community will reap the results of your extremely unfair affirmative action policies which encourages the cream of the department to seek other employment. If the department continues on it's present course of being dictated to by absurd internal and external pressures then the situation will only grow worse. Your position requires a strong, fair and dynamic individual who will not yield to pressure. An individual who has the ability and intestinal fortitude to balance the scales of justice with compassion instead of a cold hand of indifference. One who will face the principle of fairness and equal opportunity above the benefits of his own personal position.

History has revealed and rightfully so, so the county commission supported the firing of such a man when Mr. Stierheim fired E. Wilson Purdy. It's popular knowledge within the department that he was one of the most competent and professional law enforcement administrators to ever pass through Dade County.

Hopefully someday the county commission will finally recognize and take appropriate action to stop the extreme affirmative action that you and Mr. Stierheim cherish so greatly because it promotes reverse discrimination in it's strongest terms.

As a result of unwarranted exempt supervisory positions being created to satisfy your insatiable appetite for affirmative action, the departments workforce has taken the shape of an inverted pyramid.

As a result the department is completely overloaded with costly layers of management and unwarranted positions that are counter-productive. An unbiased study of the rank structure would have great difficulty in finding a valid justification for the continuance of some exempt positions which have a negative impact on efficiency. As of January 1985, the department had a total of 2,189 sworn personnel of which 571 enjoyed some time of supervisory position or almost 25% of the total workforce. This violates the theory of efficient span of control and needless to say the situation only grows worse. It doesn't take an efficiency expert to realize that if private industry worked under the same criteria, they would bankrupt themselves in a short period of time.

Reverse discrimination and ultra-liberal policies such as yours has run it's course. The days of your supervisory style are numbered as reflected by recent court decisions. Eventually the courts will re-store my constitutional rights regardless of the efforts by you and Mr. Stierheim. Your policies have denied me my inalienable right to the pursuit of happiness.

Am I to believe that all men are born equal before the law? What has happened to the basic concept of our beloved country? Justice is precious. It's not given away, it has to be fought for and earned. It is the foundation of our great country and now more than ever required constant vigilance. It was bought and paid for by freedom loving patriots and our founding fathers who dreamed of and created a magnificent country where all men could stand proud and equal before the law. To deny any citizen full equality and protection by the law tears at the very heart of our constitution. As for me, it would be a much greater gift to be a dead man than a live slave.

Your administration under your guidance has slowly, skillfully and in-tentionally placed me in bondage with it's policies as effectively as if it used forged steel shackles. The Affirmative Action Program contrived and implemented by you and the county manager has served this purpose well.

As for me, I'm as good as any man and I will never accept your perception that I'm a second class citizen and must personally pay for the sins of our forefathers. The only sin that I'm guilty of is sitting on my hands for too long and not crying out against the tide of racial discrimination that has engulfed our department. Rest assured, I remain steadfast in my refusal to forfeit my constitutional rights to enhance your personal goals. The 14th amendment states that no state may deny to any person within it's jurisdiction the "equal" protection of the laws. There is no constitutional right for any race to be preferred. We must have a "color blind constitution" if true equality and justice is to become a reality. May I suggest that you familiarize yourself with the 1964 Civil Rights Act, title 7, section J, and then if you can continue to enforce and encourage preferential treatment in good consciousness, then God help the department. Affirmative Action as you have implemented it has become an albatross around the neck of justice and totally unqualified individuals have used it as a vehicle to positions of authority with your blessings and assistance.

The U.S. Justice Department is presently addressing the U.S. Supreme Court to put an end to any form of racial preference which is exactly the position that the plaintiffs took in the landmark case of Brown vs. Board of Education in 1954. The petitioners then contended that the 14th amendment prohibits a state from making racial distinctions in the exercise of government power. Through your actions and supported by the county manager, you have bastardized the original and true intent of affirmative action. You have seemingly operated under the premise that some people are more equal than others. I personally will never accept a guilt trip from you or anyone else.

In June 1984, the U.S. Supreme Court ruled in a case involving the Memphis Fire Department that judicial relief should be confined to "only those who have been actual victims of illegal discrimination." Is justice served by punishing the son for the sins of his father? Do you entertain the "divide and conquer" concept of management?

When you recognized, legitimized and accepted the first "social club", i.e., the Progressive Officer's Club in the decision making process of the department, you started a polarization process between all ethnic groups that effectively divided one ethnic group against the other. Instead of correcting an existing problem you compounded it by accepting the Hispanic Officer's Association. Then the Female Officer's Association was formed and each organization gained the position of influence in your decision making process.

In desperation I had to found and organize the Professional Law Enforcement Association in order for the Anglo-Saxons to even be recognized as a legitimate part of the system and since we were the only ethnic group in the department without representation. The Professional Law Enforcement Association is the only organization in the department excluding the PBA, that represents every ethnic group and the only organization that's striving for total equality and equal opportunity. You have yielded without hesitation to the demands of the H.O.A. and P.O.C., giving you the posture of a weak leader.

The following is the preamble of The Professional Law Enforcement Association's Constitution. Although it is redundant in some area's that I have already covered, I'm sure you will find that it is interesting reading. You will see that it serves no special interest or group and reflects the true spirit of what America is all about.

"We, the members of the Metro-Dade Police Department, do hereby associate ourselves for the following purposes: To support and defend the Constitution of the United States and the State of Florida: To promote the cause of Professional Law Enforcement and to seek justice and equality for all; To cultivate a spirit of fraternalism and mutual helpfulness among our members; To provide legal assistance to those who are represented by the association; To expose injustices within the system; To establish high standards, pride and sense of fair play in the hiring and promotional processes within law enforcement To seek equality and to once again be recognized as a legitimate part of the system; To diligently strive to expose and eliminate discriminatory practices that erodes the basic principles from which all our freedoms are founded; To stop the tide of racial quotas and preferential treatment before it destroys the traditions of skill and excellence and to cast off the predetermined destiny handed to us by the system.

Let it further be known; That the replacement of individual rights and opportunities by a system of statistical classification based on race, color, sex, color or ethnic background is repugnant to the basic concepts of a Democratic society. To ignore the qualities and abilities of the individual is to sacrifice the great potential for innovation, for creation and for superior leadership. The Professional Law Enforcement Association embraces the 14th Amendment to the United States Constitution and seeks "equal protection of the law" as any other citizen of the United States.

We hereby dedicate ourselves to the mission of ensuring that the constitutional concept of citizenship with all attendant rights and privileges will be henceforth embraced by all people regardless of their race, sex, religion or national origin.

This is what the Professional Law Enforcement Association stands for and if it's wrong in spirit and intent, then our forefathers who drafted and signed the Declaration of Independence are to blame.

Any system including a hiring and promotional system based on race, sex, religion, culture or national origin is ungodly, immoral and cannot stand if freedom and justice is to survive in America. It must end.

Too many young American soldiers have shed blood and lost their lives on foreign shores, jungles and the rice fields of Asia for the preservation of freedom for me to stand by and do nothing when forces within our community are robbing me of that precious freedom. My soul cries out for justice and I will continue my struggle as long as God Almighty gives me life.

I pray that the Professional Law Enforcement Association will always stand strong for individual rights and ignite a fire for justice that will consume our department and spread across our great country like a prairie fire. I pray that one day justice will pour down upon the young officers of our department who have been the victims of reverse discrimination, like a great river from the mountain side. God knows they deserve it. I stand firm on the belief that right shall prevail in the end.

Recently I visited the Jefferson Memorial and I read the words of this great patriot etched in stone. The words became equally etched in my heart and a force within me demands justice and I will never accept anything less. You have denied me my pursuit of happiness and robbed me of my so-called inalienable rights. By your actions you have redefined inalienable and have apparently construed the words of Thomas Jefferson to suit your own personal philosophy.

In 1963 on a hot summer day on the steps of the Lincoln Memorial, Dr. Martin Luther King, in equal frustration so profoundly cried out "I have a dream. A dream that is deep rooted in the American dream."

I too have a dream that one day I will be judged by the content of my character and not by the color of my skin. I too dream that one day white men, black men, hispanic men, jew, catholic and protestant can hold hands and cry out together so that their voices can be heard across this great land, "equality at last, equality at last, thank God Almighty we're equal at last."

Sadly, the policies that you have implemented have all but totally destroyed department morale and particularly the morale of those dedicated officers that pursued college degrees in an effort to further their careers just to find out that education and ability are not prerequisites in the promotional process. You and Mr. Stierheim in your zeal to change the structure of the department have created a Frankenstein with suicidal tendencies.

Minorites needed and asked for a helping hand and you deluged them with handouts. Irreparable harm can be done to the psyche of any person. Especially some minority officers on the department when it's implied that they don't have the intelligence to compete for available positions by competitive examinations. You created numerous unwarranted exempt positions for the obvious sole purpose of assigning them to minorities. In doing so it was implied that whether intentional or not that they don't possess the mental intellect to compete with their peers in the competitive examination. Your policies have created a feeling of inferiority among their ranks. Actually enforcing the false belief that they lack in intellectual ability. It's a common belief that reading comprehension was deleted from the written portion of the promotional examination in order for more blacks to attain a passing score. By doing so you have again added substance to this false belief. They scrambled for the charitable give away positions that you handed out and in doing so, sabotaged black pride and their self esteem. It's imminent that positions so acquired will eventually have a strong negative impact on the operational efficiency of the department. If the process of elimination of qualified personnel continues the future of community respect doesn't seem too promising. Unless the department reviews the hiring and promotional procedures and becomes more selective in their applicants, the department will go through a period of unparallel corruption as already reflected by the recent arrest of Officer Vidal of the NorthWest District. In the department's zeal to accommodate external and internal pressures for affirmative action, standards were lowered in the hiring and promotional opportunities and unfortunately the community will reap the results. For the sake of the community and department I sincerely Hope that I'm wrong but time will tell.

Considering the direction that you and the county manager have taken the department, I can now fully understand what Plato meant when he said, "All forms of government destroy themselves by carrying their basic principle to excess, the democracies become too free in politics and economics, in morals, even in literature and art, until at last even the puppy dogs in our homes rise up on their hind legs and demand their rights, disorder grows to such a point that society will abandon all it's liberty to anyone who can restore order."

I sincerely hope that you and Mr. Stierheim have done to this department was through gross ignorance and not intentional. I personally refuse to believe that anyone would set out to intentionally and methodically destroy the structure of such a proud and progressive police department.

It must be said that Mr. Stierheim's pending resignation has been enthusiastically received by the rank and file and has enhanced morale more than anything else in recent years. Unfortunately I suspect that your retirement will also be received as joyously.

I leave the service of the department sad of heart, not for myself, but for all the present and future young men and women who join our profession in the false belief that education, hard work and dedication will have it's rewards.

END OF THE RETIREMENT MEMORANDUM

It's quite impossible to write about and describe two morons like the Director and County Manager in just a couple paragraphs. I'll try my best to continue on how they destroyed the police department but it's hard staying on that subject when there are so many idiots running around shooting off their mouth about everything underneath the sun. The more I try and understand human nature the more I love animals. Things can't be that great in our run wild society when someone commits suicide every twelve minutes and people are used for target practice by thugs in the windy city of Chicago. Now we have a school board of idiots in Minnesota declaring that it's harmful to the little children in school to display our nation's motto "In God We Trust" in the school house. It's obvious that anyone with this mindset has their head up their ass. If that's not bad enough now we have the mothers of the girl scouts forcing the boy scouts of America to delete the word boy because it is toxic to the girls in the girl scouts. Toxic??? Toxic my ass. Now the boy scouts have changed their name to simply be Scouts USA. Maybe now the sensitive little girls and their mommies won't feel inferior anymore and have hurt feelings. It probably hurts their feelings seeing the boys wearing pants instead of dresses so it wouldn't surprise me to see the mommies insist that the boys wear dresses instead of pants. Even after that problem we'll have the problem of boys and girls being physically different. The boys wearing shorts and the girls wearing panties has to be disgusting to the mommies and I'm sure they'll figure out something to do about that too. Enough of this silly ass crap. Let's get back to the destruction of the police department.

Officers who possessed strong principles of fair play and the work ethic quickly rejected their ideals and principles in order to be accepted and rise to top positions of power. It caused even the best officers to change direction and fall in with the corruption. The new organization of the department could best be compared to a septic tank because it seem that the largest lumps always rose to the top. It became common knowledge throughout the department that in order to fit in with the power structure you had to become one of the boys. It was the only opportunity you would get for advancement and accept the kiss ass concept of the department. As a result there were too many unnecessary and overpaid people sitting on their fat ass doing nothing worthwhile, while a short supply of patrolmen were busting their ass on the streets doing all the work.

It became the Rule of Thumb to promote what seem to be the biggest assholes on the department to high salary positions based on anything and everything but merit and ability. One day you'd see an officer so half witted he couldn't find his way out of the station house unless he held someone's hand and the next day he'd be promoted to a major or chiefs position. Some of them couldn't hit themselves on their ass with a bow fiddle muchless perform the administrative duties required of their new position. It takes more than a three piece suit and a fancy title to transform an asshole into an intelligent human being.

It became obvious and quite apparent that education, experience and ability were not considered in the promotional process and the result was the start of the largest and most active in house ass kissing contest that I had ever witnessed in my entire life. I can honestly say that I have never wanted or sought any position in the police department or in life that I'd resort to following someone around with my nose in their ass. After seeing what was happening to the police department it reminded me of a couple things that really gripe my ass.

Everytime I see or hear that little sawed off pimp Al Sharpton running his racist mouth off yelling "no justice no peace" I feel like stepping on him like I would a roach. You can tell that there is no limit to his stupidity when it comes to the U.S. Constitution because he hasn't realized yet that the Constitution was drawn up by a lot of old white men that owned slaves. Those old white men gave puny little Al the right to shoot his mouth off and continue to take money from the ignorant. Knowing that some old white men owning slaves gave him that right would surely set Al's hair on fire and have him running around in circles shouting that the sky is falling. Poor puny Al, like it's been said before, life is tough and it's a lot tougher when you're stupid.

Another thing that bugs my ass is to hear someone bitching about unemployment while they have two or three foreign vehicles parked in their driveway. We need patriots like that like we need a hole in our head. I have to go along with President Trump when he says "buy American and hire American." It appears to me that most of our so-called patriot citizens are doing everything that they can do to destroy the American automobile industry. When you're out for a drive notice how many people are driving foreign vehicles compared to American produced vehicles. In my observations I would say that foreign cars out number American cars by nine to one. Such patriotism, I'm convinced that the citizens couldn't careless about supporting our car industry. Being made in the U.S.A. doesn't mean jack shit to them. I personally drive a Chevrolet truck with 300,000 miles on it. It's twenty one years old and worn out to say the least and I'll keep driving it until the wheels fall off before I buy a foreign vehicle and put twenty American workers out of work. My primary concern is that American workers depend on each of us to buy American products.

Well, back to the destruction of the police department. I occasionally address some current event to get me off the depressing subject of destroying the police department that was so much a part of my life for twenty five years. During the last few years of my employment with the department I had the privilege of working with and for a fellow that was so taken up with his position and ambitions that nothing else mattered with him. I like him and thought that he did a good job even if at times I had a strong urge to kick his ass. I'll never forget those close door, confidential, confide in me meetings that we use to have in his office. Apparently he was under the impression that I was

35

some kind of dummy or something because as soon as I left his office he would call the Director and tell him everything I said. He was my private pipeline to the Director. Sometimes I would purposely discuss a truck load of worthless bullshit knowing that he would feed it to the Director. The Director was interested in what I had to say because I was the founder and president of the Professional Law Enforcement Association that was critical of the Director and County Manager regarding the way they were changing and destroying the department.

I still take a lot of pride that I personally wrote the Preamble of the Professional Law Enforcement Association's Constitution during troubling times with the department's leadership and reckless policies that were destroying a proud police department. The leadership of the P.B.A. known as the Police Benevolent Association did everything within his power to destroy the Professional Law Enforcement Association. The P.L.E.A. membership was having their membership fees deducted from their pay checks by the payroll department. The P.B.A. president that kissed everyone's ass to get the county payroll department to stop deducting the dues of P.L.E.A. members from their paychecks in the hope that it would destroy the membership and organization.

Well, it didn't work fat ass and why don't you retire and stop milking the P.B.A. and Dade County. I can only imagine what expenses you record on the P.B.A. credit card. How you get away from the charge of "double dipping" is beyond me. It's still a mystery how you get paid by Dade County and the P.B.A. for the same work during the same hours. One thing for sure you must have kissed the right ass. No doubt you'll ride the gravy train as long as you can keep your hand in someone else's pocket. No doubt you're a good Democrat. Well enough of Fatso, let's get back to more important things.

It was common knowledge throughout the department that I was an opinionated individual and stood on my personal convictions of right and wrong. I always tried my best to evaluate any and every position in a logical manner and couldn't stand gross ignorance. The director in all of his infinite wisdom gave blessings to the creation of so-called social clubs within the department that only divided the department's personnel. The black officers formed the Black Officers Progressive Club and promptly sued hell out of the county and department demanding that they be freed from bondage and given the high supervisory positions that they so rightfully deserved. Competitive examination and merit became a thing of the past. They claimed that the section on the written test dealing with reading comprehension discriminated against their culture and had to be dropped from the written examination in order for it to be fair.

After years of being subjected to affirmative action guide lines and what it was doing to undeserving white officers and myself I could certainly understand why we were simply tired of being white. The Hispanic officers caught on quick. They figured if it worked so good for the black officers then why not for them too. They formed the Hispanic Officers Association and also jumped on the discrimination band wagon with the black officers and filed their lawsuit against the county and department demanding everything underneath the sun and it wouldn't have surprised me if the ball less director would have erected a ten ton granite statue of Jose Marti in front of the police headquarters building. Well, you guessed it. Here comes the female officers. It certainly appeared that the director was in the process of giving away control of the department to the largest groups of whiners he could locate so of course the ladies got all excited. They formed the Female Officers Association and surprised everyone by continuing to conduct themselves in a professional manner. They sacrificed their clout for the sake of professionalism. I have never had anything but the utmost respect for those young dedicated female officers.

Obviously a fellow of my ethnic background was in trouble at this point. The blacks wouldn't let me join up in their organization. The

Hispanics said that I wouldn't fit in with them either. I had an obvious physical disability regarding the female club and out of desperation with no other place to turn I had to form the Professional Law Enforcement Association of Dade County. We were the only social organization in the department that opened our door of membership to everyone and were proud to have members of every ethnic background. Now you will be able to really appreciate the closed door meetings I had with my supervisor friend that served as my private pipeline to the director. I use to really laugh my ass off the way I'd sit in his office and have him pump me for information regarding what I thought of the director and county manager. I would always tell him that both of them were nothing but big assholes and I was thinking about filing a lawsuit against both of them. I really enjoyed myself feeding him a lot of meaningless bullshit for him to tell the director. I'll kiss the south end of a north bound mule on the courthouse steps and give you thirty minutes to draw a crowd if he wasn't on the phone calling the director before I could get back to my office. Of course it's probably just a coincidence but shortly after I retired my pipeline to the director was promoted to chief.

It certainly appeared that the director and county manager were doing everything they could to destroy the morale and effectiveness of the police department. I tried to convince myself that what they were doing was through gross ignorance because it was easier to accept in that light. Now I'm of the definite opinion that both of them set out to change the structure of the department in such a manner that it would eventually eliminate proven talent from the department that they didn't agree with. This same attitude runs throughout the United States and the best examples are places like the state of California and the city of Chicago just to name a couple. The liberal left like most of the Democratic party are famous for driving a city into bankruptcy and total chaos. Last year (2017) the city of Chicago had four thousand homicides and it's not even news worthy if seventy two people are killed over the weekend. A person can't even walk to the store for a loaf of bread without taking the chance of being mugged or shot to death. Of course it's run by a bunch of liberal democrats so what should we expect? Some people just can't get over anything as in the case of crooked Hillary Clinton. She's still running all over the country and even the world bad mouthing President Trump and America. It's gotten to the point that Chuck Schumer or Nancy Pelosi can't get her to shut up. If anyone observed Maxine Waters of California shooting off her racist mouth the other day in congress you'll be able to see what a real true blue racist sounds like. She's so hell bent on having President Trump impeached that's all she can think or talk about. I'd love it if someone would stick the impeachment proceedings up her racist black ass. If anyone needs to be on a plantation picking cotton it's that big mouth sorry ass racist. Hopefully her equivalent puny little Al Sharpton will be on the next row with his cotton sack picking cotton instead of yelling "no justice no peace". That's where he belongs instead of a crowded street corner talking to a flock of ignorant sheep. Sometimes I have to change the subject because reminding myself how the police department was destroyed depresses the hell out of me. Thank God we have Donald Trump as the president because if anyone can save our country he can. The best thing about President Trump is the fact that he's not a lawyer. Every lawyer and judge that I came across when I was robbed by a lying female lawyer and two couldn't careless judges has sealed my opinion of lawyers and judges. I discovered that the so called "due process" clause is a crock of shit that enables lawyers and judges to rob hell out of you. Most judges couldn't careless about what you have to say and some don't even recognize that you're in the courtroom.

It's a sad and unfortunate state of affairs but police departments throughout the United States are facing the same circumstances and losing much needed talent because those officers can't function under the discriminatory programs being implemented. It became apparent to me that the police director and county manager had a love affair with the so-called affirmative action guidelines and if you didn't agree with it then you just simply wouldn't fit into the programs in the department. At the time the law of affirmative action was applied and controlled the decision making process of the department I tried to understand it but soon realized that it in itself promoted discrimination to an unheard of scale. I was convinced that trying to apply affirmative action in the promotional process would do nothing but force the best talent out of the department. Why would anyone with experience, college degrees and merit want to remain in a department that refused to recognize them and their ability? By the way the director and county manager were running the department they created a Frankenstein monster that was surely going to destroy a proud police department in a matter of time.

Being a police Lieutenant placed me in the middle management structure of the department according to all the books regarding management. One would think that middle management personnel would have an impact on the direction and policies of the department. Not so. A lieutenant on the Metro-Dade Police Department feels like the guy that paid a quarter at the pay toilet facility to have a bowel movement and only farted. The truth of the matter is that I had no more impact on the direction of the department then the tides of the Atlantic Ocean would have been effected if I pissed off the end of the fishing pier. When any police department ignores ability then the public will reap the benefits. I have actually seen police recruits entering the police academy that didn't know the difference between "rode" and "road" or "write" and "right". Some didn't even have a sixth grade reading level and needless to say they were gladly accepted into the police department.

Whenever I attended a staff meeting I always objected to what I saw wrong but it didn't take me long that it would be best to keep my mouth shut. I never realized at the time that the director and his pals always had a habit of playing a few rounds of golf at the local country club on county time. At one staff meeting I made mention of some officers doing activities on county time that had nothing to do with police work and even heard rumors that they were actually playing games of golf on county time. That's when I realized that it was best to keep my opinion and mouth shut when it was mentioned that the police chief at the meeting had his golf clubs in the trunk of his police car. At that moment my future with the department was doomed and guaranteed by that particular police chief. He spent the rest of his career spreading the word that I was too opinionated and wouldn't fit into their program. One time I put in a transfer to the robbery section on the second floor of the headquarters building. One evening I got a telephone call at home by an unidentified person who told me to withdraw my request because there was no possible way I would fit in or be accepted in their section. That wasn't the only time that I was warned about a pending transfer request and it became obvious to me that the entire department was corrupt in some manner whether I wanted to believe it or not. It just didn't sit well with me knowing that the ones drawing huge salaries were doing nothing but sitting on their ass and trying to organize another golf game at the country club. Every now and then one of them could be seen walking up and down the hallway carrying a steno pad trying to look like he was doing something. They were so busy roaming around the building doing nothing and promoting themselves that anyone could steal al the furniture out of their office without them even being aware of it. Most of the ones holding high supervisory positions were about as useless as tits on a bull hog.

I remember another meeting of staff officers which reinforced my belief that half the supervisors in the department above captain should be fired and run off. At that particular meeting I brought a problem to the attention of a regional commander. I was constantly observing on duty police officers parking their police cars in front of a local Pizza Hut restaurant and spending a good amount of time inside playing video games while all the customers in the restaurant gathered around and watched. I suggested that it certainly wasn't appropriate and felt that a written directive was in order prohibiting such conduct. The assistant chief looked across the table at me and informed me that there wasn't anything wrong with it and besides he like playing video games himself. This is the type of mentality that controls a great many police departments today and unfortunately the situation only grows worse. This just happen to be the same police chief that keeps his golf clubs in the trunk of his police car. At least we now know that he loves playing video games and golf and no doubt he doesn't spend much time attending to police work.

For myself I have always tried to accept change because I realize that progress depends on good positive change. Of course there are always knot heads like Governor Jerry Brown of California will come along and redefine ignorance for all of us. Talk about a self serving asshole, he takes the cake and the people of California deserve him. That moron thinks more of protecting illegal immigrants and criminals then he does protecting the state's citizens. I understand that he's having a nice new home built out in the country because he sure as hell doesn't want to live in the city with all the vagrants, freeloaders, criminals, illegals and bums. The jerk has even declared that the entire state of California is a sanctuary state of all things. Some stupid people even look stupid and he's one of them. It's like movie actor John Wayne once said, "life is tough and it's a lot tougher when you're stupid."

Well, back to the department and the problem that it faces. Too often I've seen some nit wit get promoted or transferred to a new position and the first thing he does is start looking to make changes whether they're needed or not. The object was to let everyone know that he was in charge and besides there was always the outside chance that he might impress someone and further enhance his promotional opportunities. Good supervisors should always maintain an open mind to other points of view but I've seen some in upper management so open minded that they were in jeopardy of having what little brains they had falling out onto the floor. If the taxpayers ever became aware of how large amounts of money was being wasted on unwarranted high salary positions they'd march on city hall. On the other hand I doubt if the average taxpayers even give a damn. I have found to my amazement and discomfort that unless something has a direct effect on an individual they couldn't careless.

If you want to get a fast education on human behavior try and organize any group of people to support a worthwhile cause and witness a state of total confusion and conflict. For years I witnessed police officers being kicked in the ass and being discriminated against by affirmative action guidelines until I couldn't take it anymore. I stood up and told the director and his flunkies that "I was mad as hell and wasn't going to take it anymore". Being that there was no organization in the department that I could turn to for support I organized the Professional Law Enforcement Association of Dade County. It was the beginning of a new education for me. I soon learned that the officers that bitched the loudest about the conditions that they had to work under didn't have the courage of a piss ant when it was time to stand up with me and be counted. Most of the big mouths started looking for a place to hide because they didn't want to offend the ones running the department. The time to offend someone had long passed and it was time for someone to display some backbone. It became obvious to me that the ones that were suppose to cover my back were nothing but a lot of talk and were more interested in throwing me underneath the bus then protecting me. To my surprise and salvation those quiet and meek little officers who never had anything to say responded to my call for unity and displayed the courage of a roaring lion. With their help and support the organization grew strong in numbers and influence.

When I first got on the police department I recall one early morning around 3:00 a.m. I was dispatched to a black drinking establishment called "Jesse Reds" located on North West 18th Avenue just North of

62nd street to pick up a wanted subject. When I arrived I was informed that the subject was in the rear of the bar room being drunk and disorderly. I went into the bar, found the subject in a drunken state and arrested him. I handcuffed and walked him out of the bar without incident. If I was to repeat that arrest today I would have to take the entire squad of officers with me and we would probably have to fight our way into and out of the drinking establishment. Political correctness has completely changed the attitude that people have toward the police. When I retired from law enforcement respect for the police had just about hit rock bottom. Having someone trying to kick my ass was so common that I had to go back and check the job description to see if getting my ass kicked was included. No where did it state that I was supposed to get my ass kicked. Needless to say I decided that if someone was going to get an ass kicking it wasn't going to be me. If I was ever put in the position of having to kick someone's ass rest assured they asked for it and deserved it. I would deal with people on their level. If some punk treated me with no respect I would lower myself to his level so he could understand what I was saying. Over the years I got to the point that I could tell if I had a punk before me without anything being said.

After years of dealing with trash it got to where I could smell trouble and recognize trash in a heart beat. Later on I will tell you about the largest pile of trash I have ever come across and what they were capable of doing.

I'll change the subject for awhile and address the demise of the Democratic party and try to understand why some citizens spend their time bashing and trashing America. I'm one of those people that say "either love America or get the hell out." If you can't love and support America then get your ass out of the country and go live in some shit hole in South America. We have people from all over the world sneaking into our country in every possible way to get on the gravey train. Then sit on their ass and stick their hand out for all the free stuff.

Maybe it's just my imagination but it seems like all the Mexican or Central American women I see are knocked up, carrying a baby in her arms and has two or three kids following behind her.

It makes perfect sense, get knocked up in some other country but be sure to squirt out the baby in America because it's free and the new born will be an American citizen. If the American government tries to deport you for violating our immigration laws just scream that they're breaking up the family. Just keep screaming nice and loud and you'll get at least a dozen immigration lawyers coming to your defense. The run of the mill lawyers will run over each other to represent you because they'll represent anyone for anything as long as there's money in it for them. Right or wrong has nothing to do with it.

One thing for sure a condom salesman will starve to death if he thinks he can make a living selling condoms in Mexico or any Central American country. Apparently getting laid is a national past time for all those people South of our Southern border.

We have so many assholes in our country it's hard keeping up with the biggest ones. They always make a mountain out of a mole hill about something that doesn't mean shit. Just for example, at a Whitehouse meeting recently something was being discussed and a young lady happened to say "the decision didn't matter because Senator McCain was dying." A simple true statement and the news media went totally unglued over it. If I was President Trump I would require everyone attending the meeting to submit to a polygraph examination to find out who was leaking any information to the news media. If anyone refused the test I would fire them on the spot. Needless to say any hold overs from the Obama administration would not be in my administration.

For myself I don't trust anyone and abide by the rule of mafia families, "Keep your friends close but your enemies closer." When it comes to leaking information no one would be above suspicion.

Sometimes the Republican Party has a problem with loyalty, but the Democratic Party is completely fragmented to the point of having no agenda to offer the country. Why anyone would support and vote the Democratic ticket is beyond me. So far the only Democrats that have won an election are the ones that openly support programs of the Republican Party. Unless the Democratic Party wakes up and returns to the center their members may as well retire and hang it up. They are nothing but a political party of obstructionist and have nothing to offer. They are for open borders, higher taxes and more restrictions on business operations. It appears that the Democratic Party has had suicidal tendencies for the past thirty years and it's finally catching up with them.

The empty suit Obama, who never held a job in his life other then being a community organizer, did everything he could possibly do to destroy and make America like a third world country. Three things will always come out, the sun, the moon and the truth. The truth will be known when Obama's college records at Columbia University are finally unsealed and opened for the world to see. At present I have no facts but it's my humble opinion and I believe that it will show he registered into the college as a foreign student. Some people attended the same college at the same time and even took the same classes never seen or heard of him. When he was elected to be president of America the country has never experienced such a level of corruption in the federal government. Obama kicked off his campaign for president in the living room of Bill Ayers, who is a home grown terrorist that spent most of his time blowing up police stations, burning and stomping on the American flag. It should be mentioned that Obama had also gained the full support of the Black Panther Party. Ever since that young lady at the staff meeting at the Whitehouse made the truthful and innocent remark that "it didn't matter because Senator McCain was dying", the media and talk show host immediately shit in their pants. And it was absolutely terrible that President Trump referred to the MS-13 gang members as animals. One member of the television show "The Five" stated that the president should never call another human being an animal. Well, my do gooder friend who happen to be a bleeding heart liberal Democrat, let the MS-13 gang murder your son, stab him one hundred times, cut off his head, cut his chest open and rip out his heart then tell me about President Trump calling them animals. For myself calling the trash animals is an insult to the animal world. Besides cutting someone's head off, stabbing them a hundred times and ripping their heart out of their chest, another favorite past time is beating someone to death with a baseball bat after gang raping her. After being arrested they appear in court laughing their ass off about it. If anyone feels that the MS-13 trash should be entitled to a trial then they must have their head up their ass. MS-13 gang members take joy in cutting up their victims instead of shooting them. For myself I say crucify the sorry trash bastards in the courthouse square and let them hang there until they rot and the buzzards pick their bones clean. I'm a firm believer that anytime a terrorist or anyone that fits the mold of MS-13 gang is caught and convicted their families should be deported and their homes bulldozed down.

Thousands of illegal refugees pouring into our country has made America the garbage can of the world. I'm beginning to believe that the only thing that will save our country is an open and armed revolution. It was once said by one of the creators of our country "The tree of liberty needs to be watered occasionally by the blood of patriots". I fully agree with the statement and it's high time for the tree to be watered. The United States needs to suspend the Constitution for five or ten years in order to bring our country back into a sane state of existence.

As I've stated numerous times being a lawyer should disqualify anyone from holding public office. Look to Congress and you'll understand why I make such a statement. It's imperative that there should be term limits in Congress to prevent the money changers and senile politicians from controlling the country. If you want to get on my shit list just tell me that you're a lawyer. I can't stomach anyone that thinks nothing of robbing someone. Individuals that call themselves lawyers will misrepresent anything in court in order to win the case. All the lawyers that I've ever had anything to do with wears robbery as a badge of honor. Some of the dumbest bastards I've ever known are sitting on their fat ass pretending to be a judge. Most of them probably attended some Mickey Mouse law school or took graduate courses on the internet.

During my twenty five years in law enforcement I could relate stories that would curl your hair. One of my favorite topics is the death penalty and how it should be administered. Hanging and the electric chair were good and effective ways for getting rid of scum. Everytime you turn around you'll see another political asshole like the governor of New York doing something stupid. He paroled an animal that murdered two police officers and then gave all the jailbirds the right to vote. Talk about stupidity this jerk ass governor takes the cake hands down. I'm all for building gallows like they once had out West to hang scumbags and horse thieves. I'm a firm believer in public executions and doing away with parole boards. Parole boards only encourage bribery to the greatest degree.

I believe in presidential pardons but doing it in mass at the end of a president's term in office sucks. Giving pardons to one or two thousand jailbirds sucks to high heaven and there's no justification for it. Show me a city run by liberals and I'll show you a dump that use to be a city. The same thing applies to federal, county and city operations anywhere in the country. Elect unqualified morons and they'll make a beautiful city into a wasteland. Under the follow behind leadership of Obama and his friends cities like Detroit, Baltimore and Chicago went to hell in a hand basket. At present the mayor of Chicago who is a close friend of Obama has ruined the city and you can get shot just walking to the store for a loaf of bread.

The Obama administration turned the Washington, D.C. area from a swamp to a sewer and I have to question voters intelligence for actually voting him into office twice. My own family isn't immune from ignorance because a couple of them actually voted for the asshole. Some people will continue to vote with their head up their ass. Most people in congress are about as useless as tits on a bullhog and that's why corruption flourishes. A lawyer holding public office makes about as much sense as Al Capone being the Director of the F.B.I. Actually he would probably have made a better director then what we've had. The whole mess of government operations always reminds me of the way my police department operated. Corruption always seems to start at the top of any organization and spreads until it controls everything the organization originally stood for. I for one refused to stand around and do nothing when I seen the police department that I was on going to hell guided by a select few appointed by the county manager. Everyone in command positions were more interested in their golf scores then running the police department.

If the county manager had any idea what the hell he was doing a piano will come out of my ass playing "who would have thought it". From day one to the day I left county employment he still didn't know what the hell he was doing. I have always argued about requiring officers to ride in one man cars and exposing them to life threatening situations. Of course the idea of one man cars was implemented and caused by some brain dead politician no doubt. Whoever it was encouraged the idea because just look how much more coverage we can get with one man cars. To this idiot coverage was more important than some police officer getting his ass shot off. If an officer was getting his ass kicked all he had to do is request the officer in the adjoining zone to rush over and assist him. Sounds great huh, but in reality it doesn't work. First, how does the officer take control of his radio when someone is choking hell out of him and he's getting his ass kicked? If he could get control of his radio how does he speak to the dispatcher with someones fist in his mouth? The truth of the matter is that the officer will get beat down way before any help can get to him. The fact is that one man units will and does get officers killed. Just recently another police officer in Nashville, Tennessee was in his stopped car alone when someone walked up to him and blew his brains out. If there were two officers in the car the shooter would not have approached the car. Of course the news media and city fathers probably still think that splitting up police officers into one man units is a wonderful idea.

Don't put too much confidence in what the media thinks and supports. In 1948 Time magazine put Adolph Hitler's picture on the front of their magazine and named him man of the year. Hitler invaded Poland in 1939 and maybe that will show you how much the media knows. Even now the same magazine published a picture of President Trump on the cover looking down on a small crying two year old child. It was later learned that the little child was never abandoned by anyone and was used for the photograph. Just remember this is the same magazine that praised Hitler. Apparently the editor of the magazine still has his head up his ass.

It's apparent that the Democratic Party has finally died and served no useful purpose. Their entire agenda is to resist and obstruct everything that the Republican Party attempts to accomplish. It would make more sense if they replaced their symbol of a donkey with a hammer and sickle.

There's one loud mouth ignorant black representative from California who has apparently become senile as hell and should be committed. I hate to say it but the people of California deserve her. Anyone that can vote for such an idiot deserves her. If Crooked Hillary had won the election we would never have found out how corrupt tour federal government was. Everyone in charge of the agencies within the government were lawyers and that's just another reason why I can't stomach lawyers. Just recently some jerk ass lawyer sued McDonalds for five million dollars over three slices of cheese. Someone can fart on an elevator and find themselves in a million dollar lawsuit with the Environmental Protection Agency as a result of some money grubbing lawyer that happen to be on the elevator. As soon as someone tells me that they're a lawyer I hang onto my billfold. To me lawyers are nothing but well dressed thieves with a license to steal. Most of them will sue you for anything under the sun. Our country is over run by the sorry bastards and America is nothing more than a playground for unwarranted lawsuits. If you still believe in the Rule of Law and Due Process then apparently you're still asleep regarding the law. All it will take is a good screwing by the court system and you'll wake up.

As you read you'll realize that I'm a rogue writer so to speak and don't give a rat's ass what people think of me. The only person that I care about pleasing is myself. If I think someones a nit wit and deserves a good ass kicking I'll say it. Anyone with half a brain can write a book but publishers set rules that apply to non-fiction writings that takes the fun and satisfaction out of it. They require that all names and locations be changed or deleted to prevent lawyers from filing law-suits. In my particular case of robbery involving a lying douche bag lawyer and two lame brain judges explained in the book "Kangaroo Justice" you'll be able to see how easily your life can be destroyed. It really aggravates me somewhat not being able to name the sorry bastards for wrecking my life. I just hope I can outlive the sorry bas-tards and each one is buried face up with their mouth open because I intend to make each one of their grave sites my personal latrine. My soul will never rest until the bastards pay for what they have done to me. Ordinary people including lawyers and judges have to be careful how they treat other people because there's a price to be paid. Years can pass by and with some people wronged it's never forgotten and festers in their minds until they snap. Take the case that happened at a newspaper company in Maryland where five innocent people were killed by a disgruntled ex-employee. There's no free rides in life and for every committed wrong there will eventually be a response. It can be immediate or years later but rest assured it will come in due time. Some people think they are the meanest person in the valley but rest assured there is always someone that can kick your ass over your shoulders big time. I only intend to write one more book after this one which will be named "Hard Times" and be the story of my life of poverty. Hopefully I'll live long enough to get it published but sometimes I have my doubts.

My mom and dad were dirt poor when I was born and things didn't seem to get any better for them. We lived in a small country town in Northern Alabama where everyone had to scratch for a living. I never knew that we were poor until someone outside of the family told me. When I started school in the first grade I happened to sit next to the teacher's son and on that day it was rather chilly and cold. The teacher told her son to pull off his sweater and give it to me. Her son couldn't understand why and she told him because I was poor and didn't have a sweater to wear. Those were the days and a time in my life that I really believed that all people were good. As the years passed I soon realized that compassion and goodness wasn't in the hearts of all people.

We never had a television set and I use to sit on the floor in front of the radio and listen to a program called Hop Harrigan and it would always start by him saying "CX4 calling the control tower this is Hop Harrigan coming in". I'd listen to Terry and the Pirates and my favorite was The Shadow. He would always say "The shadow knows what evil lurks in the souls of men>" Life seem to be so much easier in those times. I learned early in my life that what goes around comes around and what you do today will bite your ass tomorrow. The ignorance of people has no boundaries as reflected in the mobs of protesters that demonstrate against everything that President Trump tries to accomplish. They're just plain ass Trump haters and graduated into ignorance a long time ago and will never change. They're just a sea of stupidity and their goal is to obstruct and resist President

Trump in every way possible. They always carry around their silly ass signs telling people to abolish ICE. It would be more appropriate if the signs stated to abolish the Democratic Party because they have nothing to offer America and seem to be doing everything possible to make America a third world country. Nothing bugs my ass more than hearing people trashing America. The liberal left that controls the Democratic Party supports the killing of millions of unborn babies. Planned Parenthood has murdered more human beings than Jews murdered by Adolph Hitler. Murdering babies seems to be quite acceptable to the Democratic Party as in the case of Roe vs Wade. Thank God Jesus was born before Planned Parenthood came about or Christ might have ended up pickled in a mason jar. Millions of babies have been murdered in the womb and sucked out in pieces as a form of birth control.

As far as I'm concerned and in my opinion most human beings of today haven't progressed yet to the intelligence level of most animals. For myself I have more compassion, love and respect for the animal world then I do for millions of misguided and ignorant human beings. It's been said that we all were born ignorant but some work real hard to be stupid and that's the best explanation I can offer why some people are so stupid. Just compare the behavior of animals to human beings and you'll understand why I love animals so much. Humans beings cheat and steal from each other, lie about each other and kill each other for sex. What else needs to be said?

Regarding trials for some crimes I completely agree with what the president of Russia, Vlatimir Putin, said regarding this subject. He said that some people should not be entitled to a trial. Recently we had a nut job enter a newspaper plant in Maryland and murder five innocent people with a shotgun. Giving that whacko a trial is nothing but a waste of taxpayers money and serves no useful purpose for society. Justice would have been served better if he was slowly fed feet first into a wood chipper and his remains fed into a hog pen. His family should be deported back to the shit hold country that they came from and their home bulldozed to the ground to serve notice on other potential people that are considering murder. Drawing and quartering some murdering scumbag with four horses in the middle of the football stadium at half time would also carry a good message to other people.

America is too free and controlled by self serving lawyers and politicians who pride themselves on how much money they can steal from innocent people. Every now and then I offer a tid bit of useful information to help people make it through life's difficulties. For instance if you're not banging your spouse you can rest assured that someone else is. Then we have those three little words that you never want to hear when you're getting laid, "honey I'm home," I'm convinced that more wives cheat on their husbands then husbands cheat because sexual predator men can bullshit a woman out of her panties and into the bed with little effort. They know how to bullshit a woman and before long she will give him money, flowers, jewelry and herself. He will play the woman's husband as a fool until he milks the naïve woman of everything including her self respect. A man marrys a woman thinking that she will always stay the same and a woman marrys a man thinking that she can change him. Both are completely wrong and they won't realize it until years later. Some married men and women think nothing more about getting a strange piece of ass then drinking an RC cola and eating a moon pie. It means nothing to them and they feel that it helps save their marriage which is a crock of shit.

Look at the state of affairs in America and right now that dumb ass bimbo that has lost two presidential elections is actually considering another presidential run. This bitch has to have shit for brains to even think about running again. The Democratic Party has become America's Socialist Party because of the attitude of too many people wanting everything for free. It's true as hell and has been said that

Socialism is wonderful until the government runs out of other people's money. In the 2016 presidential election we had one candidate with his head up his ass running as a socialist and millions of freeloaders voted for him. The way the lame brain protesters harass Trump supporters it's high time for them to start getting their ass kicked. Right now someone is mailing some asshole Democrats what looks like pipe bombs which don't explode. Just receiving them gives the assholes a message of what could happen. Of course all of them blame President Trump because he's blamed for everything else. President Trump isn't a lawyer and not the run of a politician and that's why people love him so. In my opinion protesters represent the trash of society and most probably have their pockets stuffed with food stamps. Their kind line the sidewalks and streets of San Francisco living in tents and boxes. They exist by welfare and what they can beg and steal. The city is wall to wall with worthless bums and trash. They are represented by sleezy elected government officials. One is a loud mouth black racist who tells her supporters to get in the face of Republicans and tell them that they aren't welcome in town. I've worked around looney tunes most of my life and this ugly broad needs medical help in a bad way. The other one hides in a closet in one of her mansions. She is a complete far out left field liberal that couldn't hit her ass with a bow fiddle. I understand that when she was a young woman she won the title of "Miss Grease Rack." Looks like she's had her rack greased a lot in her life time. Between a jerk ass governor and the two elected officials San Francisco deserves all of them. It's hard for me to believe that the voters are so utterly stupid to keep voting for them. It goes with that old say what goes around comes around.

If you think something smells rotten in Denmark, go smell Washington D.C. The place is nothing but an open septic tank filled with money grubbing lawyers on the take from everyone. They're just well dressed thieves with a license to steal. I personally don't trust any lawyer further then I can throw his or her ass.

I have discovered that the so called Rule of Law sucks for most people. Of all the lawyers that I've encountered they don't recognize the Due Process Clause in our justice system when it comes to stealing someone's money. Just look at congress and how it operates and if that doesn't wake you up nothing will.

I have friends and neighbors including some family members that have their heads up their ass when it comes time to vote. I have one next door neighbor that plastered Obama stickers all over his foreign made automobiles. Whatever happen to hire American buy American? I guess he is trying to show his patriotism because he stuck a decal of the American flag on his bumper. With his political attitude I think he'd rather die then buy an American vehicle. He's one of those people that loves dogs and from my experience there's nothing that can destroy a neighborhood faster than dogs and kids. I've said it before and I'll say it again. If you're happy where you're living stay there and don't take the chance of losing your peace of mind. Like a dummy I was happy and contented where I was living but I got a bug up my ass and decided to move into a high class restricted neighborhood and shit hit the fan. I found myself surrounded by first class assholes that bitched about everything and couldn't mind their own business. I'm convinced that one neighbor is mentally ill and the other neighbor has no balls and is completely controlled by his nosey wife. Then I have one smart ass neighbor across from me that thinks she's a real bad ass. I'll have to agree with her on one thing she does have a fat and bad looking ass on her. With a bad looking ass like hers I'll bet ten dollars to a doughnut her husband looks elsewhere for sexual comfort. I think she could have made more money selling her ass then she could ever make in her Mickey Mouse gift shop. The trouble making and lying bitch finally went out of business which was a plus for the neighborhood. She always acted like she was a clone of Ma Barker by the way she talked.

Have you ever known someone that just could never get over it? I have a neighbor that fits that mold perfectly on top of being a looney tune. Him and another neighbor constructed two large tin buildings next to their homes to operate businesses out of which was suppose to be in violation of the developments covenants which proved to be worthless and unenforceable. One neighbor has a thriving automobile repair shop and the other neighbor is trying to open a cabinet making shop.

Why the hell I decided to build and move into the development is beyond me. One thing for sure I need a good ass kicking for doing it. I saw on television the other day that a fellow got assaulted for having a small Trump flag in his yard. I'm putting everyone on notice right now regarding my flags. I have two large flag poles in my yard. One pole flies a Confederate and Florida flag. The other pole flies Old Glory and a Trump flag. If I see anyone coming onto my property to take down any one of my flags I will not hesitate one second to shoot the sorry ass bastards. I will try my level best to blow their brains out with my lever action 30-30 rifle. I will not be intimidated or harassed by misguided and ignorant young or old people. Most have no idea how a government operates or the history of our country. The ignorance displayed by protesters and even some talk show hosts regarding the Republican Party and Republican candidates is beyond any imagination. Pure stupidity and I don't know of anyway of fixing stupid. It seems to run wild throughout the Democratic Party. If you really want to see how the author got screwed, ripped off and robbed by a lying bitch lawyer and two brain dead judges, read his other book "Kangaroo Justice and well dressed thieves with a license to steal". Briefly, it's a story of how a trailer trash couple slandered another person and the court awarded them $125,000.00 for doing it. As I've said before being a lawyer should disqualify anyone from holding public office because it's common knowledge that it's just another way they can steal from the public. I don't know what all they teach in law school but "Stealing 101" has to be the main required course. If the truth was known most people voted for President Trump because he wasn't a lawyer. I've said if before and I'll keep saying it because it makes so much sense. William Shakespeare had it right when he said "The first thing we need to do is round up all of the lawyers and get rid of them". Mark Twain couldn't have said it any better back in 1866. "No man's life, liberty or property is safe while the legislature is in session". You can only imagine what takes place when you have so many thieves at the same place at the same time. All of them stealing from each other and they don't even have to wear a mask or use a gun. Before dueling was outlawed we had members of congress shooting each other. Unfortunately it was outlawed and now it's almost impossible to vote some asshole out of office.

Now try and wrap your head around what I'm about to say. Right now we have bleeding hearts and protesters raising hell because there's a couple hundred kids at our Southern border with Mexico who have been separated from their mommy and daddy. Some of the illegal adults coming into our country were dragging in kids with them and they had no idea who the parents were. It was just a good way of getting into America. The nimble headed protesters act like they're so concerned about the welfare of the children but it doesn't bother them in the least that since 1973 Planned Parenthood and abortion permitted by Roe vs Wade has murdered 50 million babies in the wombs of mothers. Whether you like it or not abortion is just another word for murder.

Now the government is conducting hearings regarding that Trump hating cockhound F.B.I. agent. Talk about a liar, this moron of an F.B.I. agent wouldn't know the truth if it hit him in the face. While banging his F.B.I. girlfriend he didn't even bother to take his wedding band off his finger. Committing adultery didn't seen to bother him in the least and his douchebag girlfriend just needed to get laid. His wife and family must really be proud of him. As if America doesn't have enough problems with empty headed protesters, corrupt public officials and illegal immigrants pouring into our country. Right now there are 14 thousand refugees from Central America marching toward America looking to work and live the American dream. They have indicated that they can't be stopped and will enter America whether we like it or not. Needless to say if we had the border wall the President Trump has been fighting for we wouldn't have to worry about a horde of people crashing into our country. As of now President Trump has ordered 800 military troops to the border to stop the horde of refugees from entering. In my opinion he should have ordered 8,000 troops to the border not 800.

The newest form of human trash have organized and call themselves "Antifa" which is apparently another word for shit. Their asshole and destructive demonstrations should be met with gun fire and plenty of it. As stated before the tree of liberty needs to be watered from time to time with the blood of patriots and it's high time that we started watering the tree.

President Trump just went to Great Britain to contact their Prime Minister and he was met by thousands of protesters carrying signs saying that he was not welcome. Their Prime Minister should remind the ignorant protesters that if it wasn't for America saving their ass in World War 2 all of them would be speaking German. It's just another example of how ignorance can take over people's minds. Of course America has it's share of ignorant people and a good part of them are politicians in congress. America is hated by almost every country on earth and we still shovel money out to them under the thing we call Foreign Aid. Talk about stupidity our congress invented the word and lives up to it in every respect. There are over 190 countries on earth and the last figure that I heard was we're paying 152 of them foreign aid. Hell, it doesn't matter to our government if you hate us we'll still shovel money to you assholes. If you piss us off real good we'll put a military base in your country to protect your shit hole country. The average person is basically a little on the stupid side which is demonstrated by most politicians.

When a woman gives birth to a male his destiny is predetermined. From the day he comes out of the vagina he spends the rest of his entire life trying to get back in. The desire is so strong he'll lie, steal, cheat and even kill for the love of it. Don't think for a second that your nice church going neighbor won't stray because he obviously has high moral standards that will prevent him from doing such a wrong. I've lived long enough to understand human behavior and nothing surprises me anymore. Always be aware of what's going on in your own happy marriage. If your loving wife suddenly wants breast implants and starts taking all the beauty treatments and joining a gym to keep in shape, wake up. Losing weight, dressing differently and finding new friends is an indication that something is rotten in Denmark and you can bank on it. I've said it before because it's etched in stone, if you're not banging your spouse you can rest assured that someone else is. Don't put too much confidence in that part of your wedding vowels "until death do us part". In my lifetime I've learned through broken hearts not to have a blind trust with anyone. I was married to my first wife for 15 years and one evening she looked at me with her loving eyes and told me that I made her skin crawl. I'll admit that I'm not the brightest light bulb in the room but I had no trouble understanding the meaning of what she said. Being blind with love and devotion I should have realized long before that remark that our marriage was a lost cause that broke my heart. Some people just seem to be a lot smarter then other people. Take for example the Polish people invented the toilet seat and years later an Irishman improved it by cutting a hole in it. Some comedian was on television this morning saying that he can't eat any kind of sea food because he can't stand the taste and it's a disgusting food. He joked about it for at least thirty minutes to the beautiful talk show host. Maybe something was wrong with him because I personally love sea food and I'll eat anything that even smells like fish.

I'm sick and tired of people trashing and bashing America. If you're not happy living in America and don't love America than get your sorry ass out and go live in some shit hole country that suits you. Speaking of trash I'm reminded of how I was robbed by two asshole circuit court judges and lying bitch lawyer in South Florida. After serving twenty five years in law enforcement I can spot a dip stick lawyer in a heart beat. I've known a lot of trash lawyers but that ugly lying bitch in South Florida takes the cake. One thing for sure there's a circuit court judge in Fort Lauderdale that she could lead around by his nose and get any court order that she wanted with no effort. One would assume that the lawyer had to be banging her sexual predator client because she never charged him one dime to represent him and his wife who fit the mold of a psychopath. Considering that the lawyer first started filing lawsuits against me in 1998 there must have been a whole lot of banging going on. The husband appeared to be a practicing sexual predator married to a psychopath who spent most of her time following him around to find out who else he was screwing.

While I was being robbed I took the opportunity to read a couple good books. Both would be real suitable reading for the lying bitch lawyer Douche Bag Mary of the Grunt and Dump law firm in South Florida. "Yellow Lake" by I.P.Daily and "Tiger's Revenge" by Claude Balls would be right down her alley. She attended a Mickey Mouse law school in 1984 and was recognized as the class dummy.

In order for readers to understand how I got robbed by so-called due process I'll re-produce the letter that I wrote to a lawyer in a large law firm in North Carolina that was hired by Douche Bag Mary to assist in my robbery based on a judgment obtained by perjury.

Dear Sir,

I have some legal problems that I need some help with before a Florida lawyer completely destroys what life I have left. In 1998 I sued a trailer couple for producing and distributing hundreds of slanderous posters with my wife's picture on them all over the county stating that she was nothing more than a diseased whore and anyone having anything to do with her should report to the health clinic for treatment. They even posted the signs on the front door of our church house where my wife sings in the choir. They distributed the posters to all our neighbors, shopping centers, local convenient store, and on all the power poles in the neighborhood. I reported it to the local Sheriff's Office and the wife immediately fled to South Florida to avoid talking to the detective from the Sheriff's Office. The husband who was still in town was contacted by the detective and admitted that he had a picture of my wife but had given it to his wife. Shortly after he gave the picture to his wife the slanderous posters started appearing all over town. I sued them for slander in a local court and a judgment of $35,000.00 was placed against them which I never made an effort to collect. When almost ten years had passed I thought that I'll go ahead and renew the judgment considering what they had done to us and our reputation. Shortly after renewing the judgment with a local lawyer in Ashville, North Carolina I was informed by that lawyer that he had received a telephone call from the trailer trash that my judgment had been satisfied by a bankruptcy court in Florida in 2003 which my wife and I knew nothing about. I called their lawyer and asked her why she never notified us about the judgment being satisfied by a bankruptcy court and she told me that under Florida law she wasn't obligated to advise me of anything. I told her that we should have been notified by her or by her clients and not doing so was inexcusable on their part.

The next thing I know she filed a lawsuit against me for "willfully and knowingly violating a court order" which was completely untrue which she admitted to me on two occasions in a proud fashion. Even at that the circuit court in South Florida accepted the lawsuit after being informed by me that the lawsuit was based completely on a lie. The court set a court date and I immediately wrote the sitting judge and told him that it was impossible for me to appear in court on the date set for the hearing due to me having a mentally ill son. I'd have to find someone to take care of my mentally ill son and enough time for me to borrow the money for the trip. I simply had to have enough time to get up the money and find someone to take care of my son in my absence.

Apparently the judge couldn't care less about my hardships and held court anyway and placed a $151,865.00 summary judgment against me for "willfully and knowingly violating a court order". I was denied my day in court which every citizen is due with complete disregard of my civil rights. I finally hired a local law firm to file bankruptcy for me because of my failing health and being in a position where it was beginning to be impossible for me to pay all the medical bills of mine and my wife's. Her insurance premiums had gone up from $189.00 a month to $456.00 a month thanks to Obamacare.

Since the lawyer started filing lawsuits against me beginning in 1998 for everything she could think of for the last twenty years I have had two heart attacks as well as strokes and the last stroke took my vision in my left eye and my right left leg from the knee down is paralyzed requiring me to use a walker to get around.

Now of all things when a large local law firm was hired by the lawyer of the trailer trash to enforce and collect the unjustified summary judgment they have done everything possible to assist in destroying my life. With all of my medical bills and health issues and being 82 years old I don't think I'll be around long enough to pay the miscarriage of justice judgment. The judgment now has reached $171,000.00 because the court raised the interest rate from 4.75% to 8% at the request of the lawyer Douche Bag Mary. I hired a local lawyer to file a bankruptcy for me but the superior court judge upheld the summary judgment against me which was based totally on perjury. My lawyer didn't hesitate to tell me that he wanted off my case and wanted it to be over.

Can you give me a ball park figure on what an appeal would cost? Is there some way I can fight the summary judgment and stop the lawyers from taking my personal property? I don't have much and even my truck is twenty one years old and spends a lot of time in the repair garage being repaired. I still feel that I'm entitled to have my day in court.

"The end of the letter"

The letter was written to the lawyer in the large law firm in response to a lis Pendens filed by the lawyer representing the trailer trash in Florida.

Shortly after the letter was written and delivered which included a copy of the slanderous poster of my wife their lawyer had me served with a lengthy interrogatory that was nothing but a sham.

Now read the letter that I sent to an obvious brain dead circuit court judge in Fort Lauderdale, Florida regarding a lying bitch lawyer that we'll refer to as Douche Bag Mary. The names have been changed to protect the guilty and insulate the author from more frivolous law suits filed by dip stick lawyers.

August 26, 2013

Dear Sir,

I just received a letter from Douche Bag Mary informing me that a hearing has been scheduled in your courtroom to determine if I should be held in contempt for not filling out papers for something that I don't know anything about. If I had opened an account someplace I'd be more than glad to fill out the information, but like I said before it's quite impossible to supply information on something that I know absolutely nothing about.

The latest lawsuit against me is even better then that. She accuses me of opening an account someplace and apparently in her client's names. I have never opened any kind of an account that I'm accused of in my entire life. One time I did borrow money on my wife's credit card to get our house out of foreclosure and that's the only time I had to borrow money.

I have written you a letter in my defense asking you or anyone else to provide me with any information regarding the mysterious account that I've been accused of opening. The request was also made to their lawyer Douche Bag Mary, but she has refused to provide any information. Is it unfair to ask Douche Bag to produce the papers of the account that she accuses me of opening just to see what signatures appears on the papers and who received the money from the loan? Some effort should be made to determine who opened the account before another person's life is destroyed by a bunch of lies.

Douche Bag Mary knows fulwell that it's quite impossible for me to drive to Florida to appear in court due to my health and lack of money for expenses. The reason she submitted papers for me to fill out is beyond me. She has been trying to shake me down for money for the past ten years and I don't see an end to it.

"End of the letter"

The circuit court judge in Fort Lauderdale, Florida probably wiped his ass with my letter or his face for all the good it done me. His ass or his face, both are the same. He needs to take his nose out of Douche Bag Mary's ass and do his job.

Don't ever get the impression that only the empty headed demonstrators are the only ones bashing and trashing America. My advice to all those assholes is if you don't love America then get the hell out of the country. You'll find Trump haters in all walks of life. To my surprise there's even one on Fox News that never misses an opportunity to criticize President Trump. His blue eyes have started turning brown and everyone knows what causes that. Him, the Democrats and all the liberals are hysterical running around with their hair on fire because they don't know if President Trump said the word would or wouldn't during his remarks to the media during his meeting with President Vlatimir Putin of Russia. The media who everyone knows is basically Trump haters and can't agree with anything President Trump does or says. My question to them is "Who gives a rat's ass what he said as long as he holds the hammer". Most of the journalist are devout close minded Democrats that will never give Trump a break and they belong to a Democratic Party that has imploded and gone to hell.

Finally the black citizens of our country have started to wake up and realize how they have been used as pawns by the Democratic Party for decades and nothing else. When candidate Trump told them to vote for him because they had nothing to lose, he was absolutely right. The leadership of the Democratic Party in the Senate and the two racist morons in the House of Representatives from California need to take their heads out of their ass and start loving America or get the hell out of the country. If they're so damn concerned about the street people and bums in San Francisco then why the hell don't they do something about it? The ignorant knot head governor of California has built himself a very expensive home in the mountains a long way from all the trash and bums living in tents on the sidewalks of San Francisco. That jerk has done nothing for the good of the state and he sure as hell doesn't want to live or associate with the people he has created. That's the simple and true explanation why the incompetent asshole is determined to get out of town when he leaves office.

Then we have a constipated senile socialist moron wanting to be president. He had a severe case of rectalitis for years and it just grew worse over time. It's a condition where the optic nerve becomes connected with the asshole and gives the person a shitty outlook on life. Once the person becomes effected they always seem to be attracted to the Democratic Party and extremely liberal for some reason. They begin to think that everything should be free i.e., college tuition, health care and even a guaranteed income for everyone. Of course this idiot attracted the support of millions of young people wanting to get on a gravey train.

The art of communication and being able to communicate with each other can never be emphasized enough otherwise we'll never have a meeting of the minds. Time and again people misunderstand the meaning of simple words causing distrust and sometimes a violent reaction. One typical example on how easily innocent words can be misinterpreted happened to me. One afternoon on the way home I stopped at the neighborhood lounge for a refreshing cold beer. The bar tender did the usual thing and placed a bowl of nuts in front of me to have with my beer. A few minutes later a very nice looking lady came into the lounge, sat down next to me and ordered a draft beer. Being the thoughtful gentleman that I've always tried to be I pushed the bowl of nuts over in front of her and simply said "would you like to eat my nuts"? That's how the fight got started and you can rest assured I will never offer anyone my nuts again.

The incident reminded me of the time one local customer took pride in his ability to identify anything that he could smell. Eventually the bar tender got tired of hearing him brag about his keen sense of smell and bet him twenty dollars that he couldn't identify objects by smell if he was blindfolded. At that one customer went outside and picked up numerous wood chips and placed them into a box. He returned and gave the box to the bar tender at which time the bar tender placed a blindfold on the eyes of the bragging customer. The bar tender held a piece of wood underneath the customer's nose and he responded "that's easy, it's birch". The bar tender held another piece of wood underneath his nose and the fellow responded "another easy one, that's pine". That procedure went on until the bar tender became frustrated and decided to do something different and really put the fellow to a real smell test. He had the bar maid get on the counter in front of the fellow and stick her pussy next to his nose. The fellow hesitated for a moment and told the bar tender to turn it over for him at which time the bar maid turned over and stuck her ass next to his nose. At that the fellow said "I know that you're trying to fool me because it's a piece of wood off the shit house door of a tuna boat". Needless to say the fellow won the bet and collected the twenty dollars.

For all your people that still believe in good old American justice let me tell you a true story. Those of you that have had justice shoved unmercifully up your ass by a court will fully understand what I'm talking about. The others will remain doubtful until it happens to them. I will briefly go through the story but if you'd like all the details read Kangaroo Justice and well dressed thieves with a license to steal. It all began when a trailer trash couple produced and distributed hundreds of slanderous posters with my wife's picture all over the county. Looking at and reading what was on the poster would make any normal person sick because it was so repulsive. A poster was even placed on the front door of our church house where my wife sings in the choir for everyone to see Sunday morning. A lawsuit was filed against the trash for the slander and libel. The court awarded my wife and I a $35,000.00 judgment against them. To make a long story short because the legal problems with the trash started in 1998 and ended in court on December 2016. My judgment was satisfied in 2003 by a bankruptcy court in Florida that my wife and I knew nothing about. On two occasions I contacted the lawyer representing the trash and was told by her that she didn't have to notify me of anything regarding the judgment satisfaction and hung the telephone up in my face. Since I had never been advised of the judgment satisfaction I had hired a lawyer in North Caroline to renew my judgment before it expired. That's when the trash called my lawyer and told him that the judgment had been satisfied by a bankruptcy court in 2003. Talk about someone really getting screwed by a lawyer I was the show-room case. I've encountered some real asshole lawyers but this sorry ass lying bitch takes first place hands down. This lying unscrupulous bitch actually turned around and filed a law suit against me for "will-fully and knowingly violating a court order." This sorry ass bitch is known as Douche Bag Mary and she knows full well that I and my wife no knowledge of the judgment satisfaction.

I wrote the judge in Fort Lauderdale, Florida explaining what had happened and the law suit filed by the lawyer was based completely on perjury. It appeared that the judge couldn't care less about what I had to say and slammed a $171,865.00 judgment against me. A judgment so high and ridiculous that anyone would think that I was a serial killer or something. It certainly stirs one's imagination on why the judge would issue such an outrageous judgment for the fat ass and lying female lawyer. No doubt they must have gone out for a drink after court for her to show her appreciation. She really lived up to her name of Douche Bag Mary considering that she was represent-ing a sexual predator and psychopath free of charge. Being that the judgment was so outrageous I hired a lawyer to satisfy their judgment.

Then Douche Bag Mary filed a summary lawsuit against me to rein-state the original judgment. She then hired a big and known law firm in North Carolina to pursue her actions in a superior court in Ashville. That proved to be my undoing because I hired a local lawyer who apparently specialized in throwing people underneath the bus. He apparently didn't like to handle any case that was too involved and expressed often that he would like to be off the case. Lawyers are expected to operate under a "Code of Silence" which means that any communication between a lawyer and his client is "privileged com-munication". In reality there is no such thing as a "Code of Silence" between lawyers because they all drink at the same watering hole and belong to the same organizations. My lawyer was hell bent on getting off my case and he continued to tell me so.

AMERICA: LOVE IT OR GET THE HELL OUT

When I appeared in court before a potted plant judge, he never even recognized that I was even in the courtroom. I had written a response to the judgment against me and filed it with the clerk of the court with a slanderous poster that had been produced against my wife. With all that information laying in front of him he still didn't recognize my presence in the courtroom or even ask me one question. The only thing I ever heard him say during the entire hearing was "draw up the order and I'll sign it."

If this is an example of justice then the careless and indifferent judge can shove it up his ass. The lawyer based his entire case on an alleged divorce between my wife and I which he was unable to prove. He couldn't produce one document proving that we were ever divorced yet the judge accepted his argument and by doing so he made my wife and I "tenants in common" instead of "tenants by the entireity" which would have protected our property and by state law no one would be able to take any part of our property because each spouse would own 100% of the property. When the judge denied us being "tenants by the entireity" he permitted the trailer trash lawyer to issue an order to the local sheriff to auction off all our personal property and home to pay off the judgment placed against us by way of perjury.

Due to the lawyers and Douche Bag Mary I had to borrow $130,000.00 on our house to pay the trailer trash for producing and distributing hundreds of slanderous posters with my wife's picture all over town including our neighbors, shopping centers, front door of our church house and on all the power poles. Hopefully I will outlive all the sorry bastards including the judge and when they die they will be buried face up with their mouth open because I intend to make each one of the grave sites my personal latrine. As far as I'm concerned each one of the bastards will have to stand good for what they've done to me and my family.

If you want on my shit list just tell me that you're a sorry ass lawyer. Being a lawyer just tells me that you're too damn lazy and sorry to work and want to spend your life robbing people. The last time I was in court being robbed by the trailer trash lawyer I couldn't understand why the 39 year old lawyer chose such a sorry profession. He had to be at least six feet tall and I found it unbelievable that they could stack shit that high. He must be good at ripping people off because I understand that he lives in the historic section of Montford which ain't cheap. In court he talked the lame brain judge into denying us the state law of "tenants by the entireity." Everytime I looked at the judge's unconcerned poker face it reminded me of the South end of a North bound mule. The judge didn't appear to know his ass from a hole in the ground regarding the state law. When he made the decision to stick it up my ass I was completely convinced that he wouldn't make a pimple on a real man's ass. He never required one iota of proof regarding anything the lawyer representing the trailer trash alleged. Always bear in mind when you appear in court that the judge is nothing but another lawyer and will probably side with the lawyer whenever the defendant is not represented by a lawyer.

They say that America is a nation of laws. That's the truth and if you don't believe it then google it. There's a law against everything you can possible think of and no doubt the Environmental Protection Agency will be after you for polluting the environment if you fart.

Being a nobody and broke what chance did I have fighting a large law firm with forty one lawyers waiting for me? Records indicate that there are 865 lawyers in Buncombe County and not one of them would take my case for some unknown reason. Nation wide there are 1,793,599 lawyers looking to screw anyone they can for money and I couldn't find even one to take my case.

Life isn't fair and you had better believe it. A man can build bridges his entire life and is he ever known as a bridge builder? Hell no, but let him suck one cock and he's recognized as a cock sucker for the rest of his life. Everyone has to find ways of entertaining themselves and I personally discovered and really enjoyed myself with rodeo sex. It was really popular with the cowboys out West. When you were going to have sex with your girlfriend, mount her doggy style from the rear then lay over on top of her back, reach around her waist as you hold her tits and whisper into her ear that her sister's tits are much bigger than hers. Then hang on and if you can stay on for ten seconds or better then consider yourself a rodeo champion.

Regardless of what you do in this life there will always be some asshole just around the corner that will criticize everything you do. In general I suppose that's why most people disgust the hell out of me. They breed like flies and think nothing of lying, stealing, cheating, robbing and killing other humans and animals. For myself I would much rather have a dog as a friend then some run of the mill human being. It really bothers me to see uncontrolled forest fires destroying thousands of acres of forest because I know that it's killing thousands of foul and poor defenseless animals. So called hunters that run around killing poor animals and calling it a sport makes me sick.

When I was on the police department I realized that human behavior couldn't sink any lower. I worked for supervisors that spent most of their time and took great joy in trying to belittle subordinates in an attempt to make themselves look smarter. When I was assigned to the Crime Analysis Section I worked for the same kind of supervisor and he proved to be the biggest asshole I ever worked under. The entire upper management seem to be in a clique and if you weren't one of the boys then you weren't in the clique. If you didn't' belong to their group then your chances of promotion was shot in the ass. One captain in the organized crime section advertised a position to be filled knowing that he had already promised the position to a good looking female officer. When I appeared for the interview for the position I asked him if I was wasting my time because I was told that he had already promised the position to the female officer. Of course he denied that he had promised the position to anyone. Two week s later after numerous interviews the female officer got the position. This particular police captain was nothing more than a barefaced liar like so many others.

You didn't have to worry about some citizen stabbing you in the back, your co-workers would do it for them. My assignment to the Shift Commander's Office for eighteen months really gave me an education. I would witness homicide detectives drinking in the Shark and Tarpon Lounge on North West 79th street until the early morning hours then turn in a time sheet for overtime. It was my responsibility as shift commander to pass out all the paychecks and it always bothered me that the county was paying them overtime for getting shit faced in a bar. I complained but I may as well have pissed in the Atlantic ocean for all the good it did. While I was in that position there was one ass kissing detective that would routinely meet a good looking female officer from the North District station. She would always show up to meet the detective in his office. They would leave the station together in a county car and be gone for hours. It always amazed me how the married detective was able to live with his conscience and bullshit his wife. He was such a devout ass kisser the sorry cheating asshole even told the captain of the section that I was checking out a county vehicle every night and leaving the station. In the entire eighteen months that I was assigned to the Shift Commander's Office I never checked out one vehicle or left the building. He was nothing but a barefaced liar and the captain believed him and wrote me up. It was the first and only time that I had ever been written up in my twenty five years of service. The sorry ass detective is still alive today and his wife never found out that he was banging his girlfriend. In retrospect I should have dropped the lip on the sorry cheating son of a bitch. At a weak moment I might still do it. The main reason I don't is because his girlfriend use to work for me and I would never want to cause her any trouble.

AMERICA: LOVE IT OR GET THE HELL OUT

Sometimes it's easy to be misunderstood even when using plain and simple terms. For example, one evening a bag boy at the local Publix grocery store was helping a shopper by pushing her grocery cart to the parking lot. The nice looking lady told the young lad that she had a itchy pussy and the young lad responded "You'll have to point it out to me because all these Japanese cars look alike." Just a simple statement and the art of communication was lost. At first things can be the same but in reality be worlds apart.

A typical example is when three men walked into a doctor's office with what they thought was basically the same problem. One gentleman had red balls, one gentleman had green balls and the third one had brown balls. The receptionist called the gentleman with the red balls and told him to go into the doctor's examination room. After awhile he came out and the receptionist charged him twenty five dollars. Then the fellow with the green balls was told to go to the examination room. After awhile he came out and the receptionist charged him two hundred fifty dollars at which time he raised holy hell and asked the receptionist why she only charged the other fellow twenty five dollars and was charging him two hundred fifty dollars? She politely told him that there was a big difference between lipstick and gangrene. The fellow with the brown balls was also examined by the doctor and paid his bill. When the day was over and he went home he found the sink full of dirty dishes, the beds weren't even made up and dirty clothes piled up in the living room to be washed. Being disgusted he told his wife just look at the house it's a total mess. She responded and told him that between taking care of the kids she didn't have time to wipe her ass. At that the husband told her "yeah and that's something else I want to talk to you about."

A man's attitude regarding a woman's vagina. He comes out of one and spends the rest of his entire life trying everything possible to get back in. Women should realize that most men are basically dogs when it comes to sex. They will lie, steal, cheat and even kill the female or any other person over a piece of ass. If a good looking woman even jogs some deserted place she's taking her life in her hands as that young woman did recently in Iowa. She was found two weeks later dead in a corn field nine miles from where she was jogging. Any man that rapes and kills a female should be fed alive feet first into a wood chipper and made into fish food. Either that or be drawn and quartered by four horses. I'm not a strong supporter of Russian President Vlatimir Putin, I strongly agree and support his belief that not everyone should be entitled to a trial.

Thank God that America finally got a shit kicking president instead of another ass kissing president like the one we had before President Trump got elected.

The federal government and the way it operated always reminded me of how "political correctness" destroyed the proud police department that I worked for in Miami, Florida for twenty five years. It seem like everything was going straight to hell and no one wanted to stop it. So called patriots lived their lives in political ignorance. Buy American and hire American doesn't mean jack shit to 99% of them. They profess to love America but still own and drive foreign made vehicles. To show their patriotism they'll stick a decal of an American flag on the bumper of their toyota. Look around you when you're on the road and you'll see that eight out of ten cars on the road are foreign made.

All the patriotic citizens are doing everything they can do to put the American automobile industry out of business. What ever happen to that old American spirit of proudness for ones country? Those patriots like Nathan Hale, who stated "I only regret that I have only one life to give for my country" while standing on the gallows waiting to be hung by the British. In these days it seems like students are not taught history or civics anymore in schools. Most students even at college level probably couldn't tell you the three branches of government. You'd think that college students would know something about

75

President Lincoln and other well known people throughout history, but they don't. For example, can they name two people that got shot in the back of the head while sitting in a theater? Of course not but for the sake of education I'll tell them. President Lincoln was shot in the back of the head while sitting in Ford's theater by John Wilks Boothe and the other person was shot in the back of the head while sitting in front of Pee Wee Herman in an x-rated movie theater. That's just a tid bit of information that might be useful to someone taking a college entrance exam.

Readers consider me a rogue writer because I don't abide by the standard rules. If I think someone is an idiot I'll say it and don't give a tinkers damn who doesn't like it. Years ago when I was just a young kid I'd ride a bus to go downtown. The fare was only five cents and I could ride all day if I wanted to. There was a sign on the bus stating that "blacks seat from the rear". I never thought anything about it because in those days we lived in a segregated society and never experienced racial problems. If anything I thought that the blacks were lucky because everyone knows that it's safer riding in the back of the bus in case of a wreck.

Recently we had a beautiful young twenty year old female murdered in Iowa by an illegal immigrant. The young lady's crime was simply jogging down the roadway minding her own business when she was attacked by a twenty four year old Mexican who was in the country illegally. It's now known that the damn animal had been stalking the young lady in the past. He attacked her and placed her in the trunk of his vehicle. When he was finished with her he killed her and put her body in a corn field miles from where he kidnapped her. He was identified because of a camera located in the front yard of a resident filming him as he followed her. The animal confessed to the crime and led the authorities to her body. It reminded me again of the statement that Vlatimir Putin of Russia once said and I firmly support. "Some people should not be entitled to a trial." This is a perfect example of someone that should not be entitled to a trial. This rabid dog needs to be dealt with in the strongest terms and for the public to see. Of course in our society he will be defended by a dozen bleeding heart lawyers who will insist that his mommy and daddy's treatment of him in his childhood caused it to happen. Not to mention how our inhumane immigration laws forced him into committing such an act. Needless to say but if he murdered my daughter I'd get to him some way if I had to throw a brick through the window of the police station in order to be arrested and placed in the same jail as the animal. Bashing his brains out in a jail cell would give me great pleasure. If he was to be punished by the state he's be given one of two options. First, draw and quarter him with four horses. Tie each one of his limbs to a horse and whip the horses to run tearing him into four pieces. The second option which I would support is to feed him alive and feet first into a wood chipper so he could observe himself coming out in pieces into a hog pen. After the hogs have eaten, deport the rest of his family and bulldoze their house down. For me it's high time to start taking lethal action against wall climbers that are flooding into our country whether we like it or not. The continued influx of people into our country from their shit hole countries will destroy our way of life and make us a third world country. They form so called caravans of people consisting of thousands marching toward our country. At least 85% of them are young able bodied men who are obviously chicken shits because they're afraid to stay in their own country and straighten it up.

Anyone voting for and supporting the Democratic Party needs a good ass kicking to straighten up their thinking process. Stupidity can be contagious because I have some family members that have their head up their ass. A survey was taken recently and it showed that 56% of Democrats supported socialism. How many of that 56% knew that Adolph Hitler was a socialist? If you're a socialist lover then don't bitch when you're being slid into an oven or marched into a pit to be shot. Freeloaders love socialism until they run out of other people's money.

Have you noticed how some people think it makes them smarter if they grow a beard and other people will really think they're intelligent. For myself I could never understand why someone will cultivate hair on their face when it grows wild on my ass. It makes about as much sense as the old saying, "The love of money is the root of all evil." People love money, but not as near as a strange piece of ass. From my experience I have come to realize that most men are basically dogs and will lie, cheat, steal and even kill for ass. May I update that old saying and change it to read "The love of ass is the root of all evil." That saying certainly applies to that senator that let a woman drown in his car at Chappaquiddick. Apparently she was diverting his attention from driving to the exciting point that he drove his car off a bridge.

It should be required reading for every misguided Democrat to understand Obama's agenda by reading his book "Dreams of my father." The day that I vote for a bleeding heart Democrat a grand piano will come out of my ass playing "Who would have thought it?" Speaking of patriotism I'm sick and tired of seeing foreign made vehicles being driven by so-called patriots. They couldn't and don't give a rat's ass if Ford, Chrysler and General Motors goes out of business as long as they can own their Toyota, Nissan, Bmw and Honda. Talk about gall, they'll stick a decal of the American flag on the bumper of their Toyota to show their patriotism.

We have mobs of millennials running around destroying historical monuments and most of them are ignorant morons that never studied history and reek with stupidity. Maybe it's time to start tearing down all the statues and road signs of Martin Luther King. Anyone caught destroying public property should be arrested and have their food stamps confiscated including all the other freeloading benefits that they receive from the government. As far as I'm concerned either you love and support America or get the hell out. Yes, that's what I said, "Get the hell out and go live in some shit hold country that you admire so much." Everytime I see the millennials demonstrating all I can see is a destructive mob of ignorant neanderthals that don't know their ass from a hole in the ground.

The beginning of America going to hell was when the government stopped the mandatory military draft. Instead of growing up, going into the military and learning a trade all the little freeloading bastards just sit around on their ass and smoke pot while still sponging off mommy and daddy. What the hell has happened to our country? Like it says on the cover, from the greatest generation to the gutter generation. It appears that the young people of this generation don't know shit from shinola and would be worthless if needed for America's defense.

They just had the funeral services of Senator John McCain and he'd roll over in his casket if everything he did was exposed. Apparently a lot of people are under the impression that he was a saint or something, but the history of his life shows otherwise. He was an okay guy but had the weaknesses of just an ordinary man. He may have been registered as a Republican in name only because his undying hatred of President Trump was always obvious. When the Bill went on the floor to repeal Obamacare he voted against the repeal killing the only chance of getting rid of it. No doubt his hatred for President Trump influenced his vote and that was more important to him then the people suffering with Obamacare. For myself in particular, before Obama took office I was paying $189.00 a month for medical insurance for my wife. After Obama took office the premiums when up to $456.00 a month. The premiums were too high for me to pay and I had to drop her insurance and each year I was penalized $1,400.00 for not having insurance on my wife.

Something that really bugged my ass about Senator McCain's funeral is the fact that Sarah Palin wasn't invited. Of all things before he died he made the statement that he regretted making her his running mate during the presidential election. McCain refused to permit Palin to attack Obama and his terrorist friends and it cost him the election. Sorry John, but if you had turned Sarah loose she would have made you president.

Hopefully some of you will remember the so-called War on Poverty. This was nothing but a program designed for the destruction of black American families by keeping them dependent on government hand-outs. The black people fell for it hand over fist and supported it by continually voting the Democratic ticket. At last the black population seems to be waking up to how they have been used by the Democratic Party for decades. President Trump has done more for blacks in two years then the Democrats have ever done for them.

It's high time for the ignorant assholes that tear down and vandal-ize statues of our country's history to understand that destruction of public property is a two way street. Whenever a Confederate statue comes down so will a statue of Martin Luther King.

Regarding college attendance not everyone should go to college because some just don't have the required intelligence. I personally believe that there is a correlation between genetics and intelligence but we'll explore that question later on in another book not writ-ten yet. A percentage of college students just don't have the mental ability to fully understand some required subject matter. At present college students owe the federal government five trillion dollars that has been paid out for their college tuition that the taxpayers will prob-ably never get paid back.

If any of you have a legal problem and think that you don't need a lawyer to represent you in court you had better think again. Courts are completely run and controlled by lawyers which should place you on notice that the only way to fight and survive in a crooked court system is by having a crooked lawyer. In my particular case I was robbed by an incompetent judge assisted by a crooked lawyer. The judge seemed to careless about right or wrong and didn't even recognize that I was even in the courtroom. With my lengthy written response laying in front of him on his desk he still neglected to even ask me one question. The lawyer representing the trash never presented one document supporting his allegations and the potted plant judge just sat there with a dumb look on his face as if he didn't understand what was being said. He ruled against me and denied me the protection of the state law "Tenants by the entireity." The Superior Court judge was a real asshole and totally unqualified to be a judge or even a run of the mill lawyer.

Justice under the law? My ass, his justice cost me a $130,000.00 mortgage on my property and I had to pay the trailer trash $125,000.00 for producing and distributing hundreds of slanderous posters with my wife's picture all over the county, to our neighbors and on the front door of our church house. Thanks to the asshole judge that didn't know his asshole from a hole in the ground. That sorry ass Superior Court judge knows who I'm talking about and hopefully the sorry bastard will develop a terminal disease or get run over by the bus that he threw me under. If I'm that lucky I'll also use his grave site as my personal latrine.

Some people just don't approve of the way I express myself and bitch because I don't play by the established rules. I don't sugar coat anything and if it offends you then put the book back on the shelf and let someone else read it.

If any of you ever need a lawyer be sure and stay the hell away from the Grunt and Dump law firm located on West Broward Blvd otherwise you'll probably bump into Douche Bag Mary who is a member of the law firm and that bitch will screw you to heaven and back. Take it from me that lying sorry ass bitch will lie like hell and do everything possible to throw your ass underneath the bus. She'll give a circuit court judge anything he wants if he'll give her his signature on a sworn affidavit. That bitch would have me subpoenaed for a court hearing ten days after the hearing was held. After investigating her last trailer trash clients it was obvious that she had to be accepting peter for payments. Her husband worked in the same office and was apparently blind to what was going on. I can only imagine all the positions that you can get in on top of an office desk. She isn't very pretty but who the hell looks at someone's face when there's so much concentration between a hole and a pole? The trailer trash didn't have any money so he had to pay the legal bill someway and besides even ugly people need sex too.

Talk about ignorance, it seems like everytime I turn around I hear of another Democrat endorsing socialism. Apparently none of the assholes realize that Hitler was a socialist or do they even care? The Democratic Party is so desperate at the time being they would probably nominate a clone of Hitler if they thought it would win them the Whitehouse. Right now it would make good sense if they dropped the donkey as their symbol and used the hammer and sickle instead.

Speaking of Hitler, he was determined to destroy the Jewish race and killed them by the millions. He put them in ovens, gased them, shot them in large open pits and buried them. Killing small children and babies were no exception. Here in America we perfected the idea of annihilating another race of people. The first thing you have to do is convince a group of people that they have a constitutional right to do a particular thing as in the case of Roe vs Wade. That way millions of babies can be murdered in or out of the womb and it's quite acceptable. On top of legalized abortion or murder by any woman, we now have Planned Parenthood to do it on a massive scale. If I was a black person I would really be suspicious of that operation of killing babies and whose idea was it? Thousands of black babies are murdered each month with no effort at all. Is there some kind of motive and hidden conspiracy to eliminate the black race like Hitler did to the Jews? If the possibility does exist then Planned Parenthood is doing a job of it. Just the thought of murdering little unborn or born babies makes me sick to my stomach.

As a former police officer I had to go to the Medical Examiner's Office on occasion and would see little unborn babies preserved in mason jars. Although they were tiny little unborn babies they were perfectly formed down to their tiny little fingers and toes. How any woman could look at an unborn little baby and still have her little baby killed is beyond my comprehension. Abortion is simply another word for murder. When I saw the little baby preserved in the mason jar the first thing that came to my mind was "Forgive them Father for they know not what they do." Some women have an affliction known as peanut butter legs that are too easy to spread and most men find it impossible to keep their dicks in their pants. As long as women use murder as a form of birth control the problem will only grow worse. Instead of liberal and black congressmen shooting their mouth off about President Trump, they should be trying to stop the genocide of the black race. To me it seems almost hopeless to stop because someone has already convinced women that it's their constitutional right to do whatever they want with their bodies including killing their unborn so it will continue until the Supreme Court rules otherwise.

Men are basically like dogs when it comes to screwing and would screw a knot hole in a fence if given the opportunity. Like I've said before humans breed like flies and it's expected that there will be nine billion people on earth in the near future which could be avoided if people used their heads more if you get my drift. The people that Hitler murdered is just a drop in the bucket compared to how many human beings have been murdered by so called abortion. Speaking of abortions contact the law firm of Grunt and Dump in Fort Lauderdale, Florida and contact a female lawyer by the name of Douche Bag Mary and you'll be able to see what a real abortion looks like. That sorry lying bitch represents what an abortion looks like if it survives because the best part of her ran down her mother's leg when she was being conceived. She wears perjury as a badge of honor and discovered that she could get anything she wanted from a horney circuit court judge. Lying under oath apparently didn't mean too much to either of them. Giving a client or a judge a blowjob wasn't that big of a deal if it served her purpose. I understand that she could put Linda Lovelace to shame and deep throating was a piece of cake.

They say that lawyers take an oath that they will never misrepresent anything in a court of law. If anyone believes that bullshit then they'll most likely believe in Santa Claus and the Easter Bunny too. All the lawyers that I have dealt with seem to be born liars and lying under oath or otherwise is just a way of life with them. If anyone thinks that any conversation between them and their lawyer is privileged communication they had better think again. Lawyers don't recognize the "code of silence" and will blab everything you talk about to other lawyers and all over town. Like I've said before they all drink at the same watering holes, belong to the same organization and routinely trade information regarding clients among themselves. For myself and my experience with lawyers I wouldn't trust one any further then I could throw his or her ass. Why anyone would want to be part of the profession of legalized thieves is beyond me.

When I refer to the gutter generation I direct that remark to the present general population and certainly not to our military and law enforcement personnel. I served eight years in the United States Naval Reserve which was in the sixth fleet and the Construction Battalion better known as the Sea Bees. No one has more respect for our men and women in the armed forces than I do.

Now let me tell you about something that bugs my ass. I live in Western North Carolina and everytime the weather forecast says that it's going to snow every jerk in the country side will run like hell to the grocery store and buy all the bread, milk and bottled water that they can carry. Then all of them will race to the gasoline stations to fill up their vehicles, gas cans and whatever until the station runs completely out of gasoline. If the weather channel says anything about a hurricane being some place in the Atlantic Ocean, the jerks go completely out of their minds buying everything in the grocery stores and running wildly with their head up their ass. You'll see every clown in town at the gasoline stations pumping gas into a dozen containers to take home. All the stations start shutting down because they're pumped dry. Then you have some idiots blaming President Trump for causing the hurricane.

If you find it hard to believe that our country has wall to wall morons, turn on television shows like the View and Good Morning Joe. One moron hopes that President Trump dies and another moron says that Trump has done more damage to America then the Arabs when they destroyed the Twin Towers. The fellow making that statement has always looked sort of stupid and proved it by running his over paid mouth. Apparently a person has to have the mentality of a turd to qualify being on one of the far left television shows. In my opinion it's time for people that love America to start kicking some liberal ass. If you don't love America get your worthless ass out and go live in some shit hole country that you admire so much and deserves you.

America's entire Rule of Law, Due Process and Justice System should be reviewed and evaluated especially in the area of punishment. As I've stated before not everyone should be entitled to a trial. There are some murdering scum that should be fed into a wood chipper alive and feet first so they can see themselves being shot out in pieces into a hog pen. Putting a murdering bastard in jail for thirty or forty years isn't punish enough in my opinion. According to the Supreme Court it's cruel and unusual punishment to deny an inmate pussy so they are entitled to conjugal visits in jail. Sometimes I think I'd have more luck at getting laid if I was in jail. Considering everything that a prisoner is entitled to and exposed to in jail it doesn't seem that bad being in jail. After a prisoner has been in jail for a few years he becomes institutionalized and you can't drag him out of jail. Maybe that's why there's so many repeat offenders. On the outside you have to work and scratch for a living to survive while the people in jail only have to sit on their ass, play basketball, watch movies, visit the book store and eat three meals a day to survive.

Thinking about writing a book? It's not that much fun because you have to refrain from using a person's real name when you call him an asshole to avoid law suits. Assholes destroyed the working environment of the Dade County Sheriff's Office in Miami, Florida and hopefully you have read my retirement memorandum in the beginning of this book that I submitted to the director of the department almost thirty five years ago. In the memorandum I predicted that the department was going to hell if they continued applying the concept of affirmative action and disregarding ability.

Today we have a situation in our country where one political party, the Democratic has completely imploded and has nothing constructive to offer to voters. When Obama was in office he more than doubled the national debt and thought nothing of making deals with enemy countries and running all over the world apologizing to everyone for America's arrogance. He proved time and again that he didn't have the competence to run a lemonade stand muchless a country. President Trump came along just in time to save our country apparently to the regret of the Democratic Party.

The evening time of my life seems to be the best way of describing the little time that I have left on earth and I'm looking forward to being with my family that I have missed so much. If I'm able to pay off my house mortgage and get my books written and published I'll be ready to join my family. It seems like when you get old and crippled you lose your zest for life. Take some advice from a crippled old man who shares his experience and wisdom of life with you. Don't ever become too friendly with your neighbors because it will breed contempt in areas of disbelief. The only way of avoiding trouble and major problems is to keep to yourself. Familiarity breeds contempt, bank on it.

My nerves must be completely shot because everytime I hear a sharp noise I jump. Sometimes it seems like it's getting worse because all morning I kept hearing tiny little voices singing "When the log rolls over we'll all be dead." After searching every room in the effort to see where the singing was coming from, I finally looked in the bathroom and there it was. Four little flies sitting on a turd in the toilet singing their little hearts out. It reminded me of the television show The View or maybe it was Good Morning Joe on MSNBC.

Then we had some douche bag making sexual allegations against the Supreme Court nominee Brett Kavanaugh, in an obvious attempt by the Democratic Party to keep him off the Supreme Court. The Democrats were desperate and were doing everything possible to stop him from getting on the court. We had Ugly Maxine running around shooting her racist mouth off and encouraging everyone to harass every Republican that could find. When I was a young man in Alabama working the cotton fields I worked with a black woman that looked just like her. I wonder if it could have been??? No, the only thing she seems good at is picking her nose and fat ugly ass. The people of California deserve her.

They say that you should never dislike or have hatred for anyone. Well, that's easy to say if you've never been a victim of someone trying to destroy you. I've been a victim for the past twenty years by a filthy trailer trash couple. The husband is a sexual predator and his ugly fat wife is a true psychopath. I not only hate the trash I despise the very ground they walk on. The husband wouldn't make a pimple on a real man's ass and his wife wouldn't even be a half way good cum receptacle if someone could stomach her. Like I've said before

I write in a direct fashion which is not practiced by many authors. When it comes to writing there are no rules as far as I'm concerned, only honesty and truthfulness.

Why the hell do I get the impression that most of the millennials attending colleges and protesting everything under the sun produces an image of a neanderthal? Doesn't it make you wonder why Obama had his records sealed at Columbia University? When he was attending school why didn't some other student ever see him? How come not one female ever dated him? Could he have enrolled as a foreign student? Being a nobody how did he get the money to attend college and set up residency in Hawaii? The first picture I saw of him he looked like he was smoking a joint. I'm still not convinced that he was born in the United States and suspect that he might have been born in Yeman. His birth certificate states that he was born in a hospital in Hawaii, but when it states when he was born that particular hospital hadn't even been built yet. When his college records are finally opened everyone will be able to see his hidden past and know the truth.

The Democratic Party was so hell bent on stopping Brett Kavanaugh from getting on the court they even had some douche bag woman testify that Kavanaugh touched her ass thirty six years ago at some drunken party that she was at while only fifteen years old. At the time Kavanaugh was seventeen years old and flatly denied that it ever occurred and he didn't even know her. The woman couldn't remember the date, where it was to have happened and how she got back home. My question is why the hell was she attending a drunken party at fifteen years of age and if she was sexually assaulted then why didn't she report it to the local police?

Then another douche bag pops up and accuses Kavanaugh of exposing himself over thirty years ago and admitted that she was completely drunk on her ass. At first she couldn't remember who it was that exposed himself but after talking to the Trump haters in the Democratic Party for six days she suddenly remembered that it was Kavanaugh. Anyone with half a brain should be able to see that the Democrats were conducting a smear campaign against Kavanaugh to keep him off the Supreme Court. The two douche bags making the false statements against Kavanaugh would say anything to please the Democrats in their effort to destroy Kavanaugh. I'm an authority on recognizing douche bags because I've been dealing with a lying douche bag lawyer since 1998. Look at how Kavanaugh was treated and then tell me that life is fair. Well, take it from an authority, life is not fair. Just like I've said before, a man can build bridges his entire life and he's never known as a bridge builder but let him suck just one cock and he's known for the rest of his life as a cock sucker.

All it takes to destroy a man's life is for some female to accuse him of touching her ass. Whether it's true or not doesn't matter because he's guilty until he can some how prove that he's innocent. His life and reputation can be destroyed based on a lie and most likely there's not a damn thing he can do about it. The entire Kavanaugh incident has put me on a guilt trip considering my past behavior. It's high time that my past indiscretion be brought to light and I be submitted to the rule of law just like anyone else. Maybe the F.B.I. will investigate my disgusting behavior and bring it to the attention of the local police. When I was in the ninth grade in junior high school I had a teacher keep me in after school to clean the blackboard and dust the erasers. One thing lead to another and before I knew what was happening she had pulled my pants down and her dress up. Within a few minutes I found myself touching and feeling her ass. It was wrong on my part and I feel that I should be punished for my disgusting behavior. Just because the teacher was giving me a blowjob at the time I was playing with her nice ass is beside the point and had nothing to do with it. I welcome a full scale investigation on why I didn't exercise some self control instead of playing with the teacher's ass. Unlike Kavanaugh

I was guilty as hell and by the time I was seventeen years old I was drinking beer and chasing girls, a disgusting lifestyle.

Speaking of Kavanaugh, I see where there was a large group of demonstrators in front of the Whitehouse protesting the confirmation of Judge Kavanaugh to the Supreme Court. Most of the protesters were loud mouth young females that appeared to be a little on the stupid side. They are scared to death that someday in the future Roe vs Wade will be over turned and they will lose their right to abort or kill their unborn child. In my opinion before any woman can have an abortion they should be required to look at an unborn baby preserved in a mason jar which they can find in almost every medical examiners office. I've said it before and I'll keep on saying it until hell freezes over. Abortion is just another word for murder. It's a sad state of affairs when murder is used as a form of birth control.

My advice to senators and everyone else is simple and appropriate. If a loud mouth half witted female gets in your face yelling about Kavanaugh or anything else, the instant that she touches you punch her lights out. She is no doubt the product of a busted condom and the best part of her fell on the bed sheets.

Life can really be a bitch sometimes and it seems like I'm confronted with one mountain after another. I'm always reminded of the song that singer Eddie Arnold use to sing many years ago. "This time Lord you've given me a mountain that I may never be able to climb." At my old age sometimes it seems like I'm in a race with death and my only hope is that I can get my books published and on the market before I lose the race. Everytime I turn around someone on Fox News has written a book and it's shown and talked about on national television a dozen times. A nobody like myself has to scrape up money and pay to get it advertised on line with Barnes & Noble and Amazon if we're lucky. An unknown author doesn't have the chance of a snowball in hell of getting free national advertising like television hosts do.

The question always comes up do grown men cry? Hell yes we cry when someone destroys our life as in my particular case which is explained in the book "Kangaroo Justice and well dressed thieves with a license to steal." Do lawyers lie and misrepresent things in court? You bet your ass they do. Does a defendant stand a chance of winning in court if he doesn't' have a lawyer? Hell no and the court looks at it like taking candy from a baby. Being in law enforcement for twenty five years some of the biggest assholes I've ever known were lawyers and judges. Don't be overly impressed by a judge because he or she is nothing but another lawyer doing nothing but sitting on their ass and drawing a big taxpayer salary. The sorry bastards robbed me of everything and put me in the poorhouse. Between the lawyers, judges and some trailer trash you'll never believe how I was crucified. Between a sexual predator, a psychopath and four officers of the court they buried me. At present the trash attends a Baptist Church in Plantation, Florida and wrap themselves in a cover of Christianity to conceal what they really are and to avoid the law.

If I haven't learned anything else in life I've learned that what goes around comes around. That sorry trash couple and their lying ass lawyer will eventually get what's coming to them someday and hopefully I'll still be alive to enjoy it. For some reason it seems like everyone involved in the court system doesn't really give a shit about what is right and wrong. I've written to the jerk ass circuit court judge that slept through my hearing and even to the clerk of the Superior Court and none of them will even answer my letters. It just goes to show you how concerned they are about an injustice. The presiding judge on my case either didn't understand the state law or was in the pocket of the lawyer presenting his case. He denied me the protection of the North Carolina state law pertaining to "Tenants by the entirety" which prevents anyone from taking my property because each spouse owns 100% of the property. The judge was wrong with his ruling and I told him so which he ignored most likely because he couldn't justify his ruling. In order to get the entire story of how you can get robbed by so called Due Process read the book "Kangaroo Justice" and you'll see how easy it's done by lawyers and without a gun.

It burns my ass to see a mob of brainless protesters harassing someone because of their political position. When I was in law enforcement water cannons were used to disperse unruly rioting mobs, but in retrospect that was a waste of good drinking water. The perfect solution today would be to still use the water cannon but instead of good clean drinking water hose them down with raw sewage straight from residential septic tanks. Rest assured getting soaked down with human body waste will cause the protesters to forget about harassing anyone and destroying property because they'll be more interested in running like hell to keep from being hit by a flying turd.

A little advice for any of you even thinking about writing a book concerning how you've been railroaded and destroyed. You'll discover that most people don't give a rat's ass about your problems and what has happened to you so give the adventure plenty of thought. Writing a book is one thing but getting it sold is something else. The only way to sale the book is to advertise it in every possible way and that will cost you through your nose. It would be ideal to have your book placed in stores so potential buyers can see it, but that's another hurdle in itself to overcome. I see hundreds of books on shelves in stores for people to examine but trying to get your own book there is almost impossible. A celebrity can fart and write a book about it and you can bet the farm that it will be on the New York Times best seller list within a week or so. It just enforces the fact that if you're a nobody you're most likely and simply wasting your time and money.

Boy, has my opinion of Senator Lindsey Graham changed. At first I didn't approve of him but was I ever wrong. After seeing his comments during the Kavanaugh confirmation hearing and his support of President Trump he has become my hero. I would love to see him run for president after President Trump leave office. Him as president and President Trump on Mount Rushmore would be perfect.

Now we have thousands of people from all the shit hole countries in Central America marching toward our Southern border with Mexico with the attitude that they're entering America whether we like it or not. When they start climbing over and crashing through our border walls then I know of a real effective way of stopping them but it wouldn't be accepted by our bleeding heart citizens. Rest assured there will be dozens of jerk ass lawyers licking their chops in glee waiting to represent everyone of them. Of all things the marching mob has obtained a lawyer already and are suing President Trump for violating their constitutional rights. That's just another asshole lawyer for you. The idea that the mob is seeking asylum is nothing but a lot of bullshit. They appear to be nothing but a mob of chicken shits fleeing from their country because they're too scared to straighten up their country. They don't like the living conditions in their shit hole countries and decided to move into America and enjoy the good life. Needless to say if our country doesn't stop the unchecked flow of refugees into our country America will become a shit hole too.

It's beyond me why anyone would support the Democratic ticket and support sanctuary cities, open borders, higher taxes and refuse to finance the Southern border wall. It amazes me how some people work so hard to be stupid. I could keep writing until hell froze over and it wouldn't do any good because you just can't fix stupid.

The End

www.ingramcontent.com/pod-product-compliance
Lightning Source LLC
Chambersburg PA
CBHW070745280626
47162CB00017B/2356